Self-Portrait

with

Russian Piano

Self-Portrait

with

Russian Piano

WOLF WONDRATSCHEK

Translated from the German by Marshall Yarbrough

FARRAR, STRAUS AND GIROUX

New York

Farrar, Straus and Giroux
120 Broadway, New York 10271

Printed in the United States of America
Originally published in German in 2018 by Ullstein Verlag, Germany, as
Selbstbild mit russischem Klavier
Publication arranged with Regal Hoffmann & Associates LLC in conjunction
with Literarische Agentur Michael Gaeb
English translation published in the United States by Farrar, Straus and Giroux
First American edition, 2020

Library of Congress Cataloging-in-Publication Data
Names: Wondratschek, Wolf, 1943– author. | Yarbrough, Marshall, translator.
Title: Self-portrait with Russian piano / Wolf Wondratschek ; translated from the
    German by Marshall Yarbrough.
Other titles: Selbstbild mit russischem Klavier. English
Description: First American edition. | New York : Farrar, Straus and Giroux, 2020. |
    Originally published in German in 2018 by Ullstein Verlag, Germany, as
    Selbstbild mit russischem Klavier.
Identifiers: LCCN 2020012317 | ISBN 9780374260491 (hardcover)
Subjects: LCSH: Pianists—Fiction. | Dissenters—Soviet Union—Fiction.
Classification: LCC PT2685.O45 S4513 2020 | DDC 833/.914—dc23
LC record available at https://lccn.loc.gov/2020012317

www.fsgbooks.com
www.twitter.com/fsgbooks • www.facebook.com/fsgbooks

10   9   8   7   6   5   4   3   2   1

**GOETHE
INSTITUT**   The translation of this work was supported by a grant from the
Goethe-Institut in the framework of the Books First program.

Does chance know what it wants?

CONTENTS

I

HANDSHAKE WITH A DEAD MAN?

At the coffeehouse. Every table occupied. Every joke told. Every newspaper read. Foreigners and locals. The waiters dance. The air a lit cigar. At my table a Russian, a piano player in his youth, a forgotten celebrity. He has made his peace. Moscow, London, Vienna. Every distance bridged in the lines of a poem, every room fused together into mystery. I tried it, a sober accounting, a sunny recollection, but I failed. In the end it's hotel rooms that you remember, more than concerts. A too-firm handshake. Pretty women who knock and then apologize, they had the wrong room. A suitcase with a broken lock. The Eiffel Tower in the fog, for two days you couldn't see a thing. And of course you knew: art can't do a thing, and it can't do a thing about it.

It's unbelievable how useless a man can become, a man like myself, who ends up slipping into a gap in memory, no shoes, no dream. His right hand, more paw now than hand, plays with a cigarette, which the doctors have prohibited him from smoking. His heart. He has it in writing. You will die. That, he answers, is what I'm hoping for. And no music, not a single note. Church bells, yes, the way they would sound in the villages of my home, the home of my grandparents, my aunts and uncles. Summer holidays, I remember, long short weeks. Caves I didn't dare set foot in. Chickens that bled to death in your hands. Waiting for a storm. Gathering wood for a fire, which of course was forbidden, but the man who went riding past didn't mind; he was completely caught up in the song he was singing. You didn't have to be a good boy, you could stay up late and listen to the stories the adults told each other. If you fell asleep, the taste of sweet wild berries still on your tongue, someone carried you off to bed. Happy life! Standing barefoot in the mud. Falling from trees into the softness below. And climbing back up. Again and again, don't stop! There were women, young strong women at work in the fields, I was ashamed to look at them. How old was I when I started having thoughts that weren't the thoughts of a child? Oh yes, already they were calling me, girls, brash, red-cheeked girls, they had been hiding! I gathered what I could find, threw it away again, kept walking. Herds of sheep. Wagon tracks in the sand. Wandering fortune-tellers, young and old, who, because the future wasn't in high demand, also traded in pearls and rare roots. My first white and black keys, an accordion. Blue kerchiefs, the color of love. Come to me again, I'm thinking of you. Then the Germans came. They didn't take our money, but they took our soap and matches. Death came, and there was no one left to explain it. The old who were still alive were no longer speaking. People who went to bed didn't get up again. If there was any singing at all, it was only in our heads, in secret. No candles burned before our icons, not for a long time. Love was warming each other's hands. In Leningrad, no one got out and no one got in. A city held captive to hunger. The safest place, and what a joke this was, was Siberia.

I hear a man talking, a man I've just met, whose manner of speaking, in this language that is foreign to him, itself sounds foreign, a fragile house of cards that he takes great care to protect, even from his own breath. This is the sound of words going uphill. And another thing, which makes it no easier to understand him: his mind wanders, his thoughts get scattered. He hears the ice breaking in the canals, hears shots being fired at bears, hears the wrong notes that he, inexplicably indisposed, once played in Paris. It's a skill, I think, you have to practice, you have to learn to give him time.

After draining the glass of water into which, without his noticing, ashes from his cigarette have fallen, he wipes his mouth dry and looks at me, as if I had given him a clever answer to a question he didn't ask.

I look forward to it, he says. And it should rain, I always loved rain. It should rain for a long time. It should rain till it gets dark, till the stars come out. God I don't believe in. I am a believer of a different, older kind.

II

DO WE NOT GET TO LIVE?

I arranged to meet with the old Russian. He suggested an Italian restaurant, not too far from his apartment.

Through the window he looked like a beggar. He was smoking. He was tired. Although he wasn't allowed to have coffee, he ordered one, which cheered him up. The act of breaking a prohibition was always guaranteed to lift his spirits. My heart loves my follies. Not all of them, but this one and a few others, and it forgives me for them, I hope. It's still going, still keeping the beat, it never drops out. Sometimes, it's true, it threatens to stop. The worst time, he said, was back in Paris, when between rehearsals for a concert he had sought out the grave of the Romanian pianist Clara Haskil in the Montparnasse cemetery. There she lay in her grave, and there he stood feeling useless. She knew more than I did. I didn't know what it was that she knew. I only knew that it was important to know it, and that I didn't know it. A secret—yet another, if we're talking about music. And it's interesting, to hear something without being able to understand it, and how much music have we all heard in our lives, good, marvelous music, brilliantly performed. And still! His heart ached. It was she he admired, more than just about anyone else who'd ever sat at a piano, but he kept this to himself. To his regret, he had never seen her in concert, and of course had never met her in person, no, though the latter he didn't really regret, since he wouldn't have had the words to express his admiration for her, and to try to shake her hand would have seemed an impertinence to him. But there was always a gulf between them, they were kept years and kilometers apart. He was fifteen and had only just arrived in Moscow to study when Haskil died in Belgium, though she was buried in Paris. She slipped on a staircase, I think, she never recovered from the fall. A moment's carelessness, which she would never have allowed herself at the piano. What are you supposed to make of it? Do we not get to live?

It didn't mean much back then, neither to him nor any of the other students. That changed when he discovered her recordings on his own and wanted to know everything about her life, her training, her career, her performances. From then on, it was almost as if he loved her, as if he loved the modesty with which she had appeared before her audience, the greatness of this modesty. It could make you ache, how small she wanted to be, how she managed to escape into simplicity without betraying the music. Music isn't a room you get to repaint. Did she speak Russian? Did she speak at all? Did her hands get cold before every appearance, too cold for Mozart, who would then warm them for her? There were doctors in her life back then, not yet any in his.

Oh right, something else I'll never forget, Suvorin said abruptly, and in his thoughts he was back in Paris, in the early years of his life. When I visited her grave, there was a cat lying there, it didn't pay me any mind, didn't even look at me, just went and stretched out on the gravestone, and in such a way that it covered up the death date with its little head, as though it wanted to trick the world, no, better yet, to prove the world wrong, to make it as though her death hadn't happened. Everything else, her name, the date and place where she was born, all that you could still see. Strange, isn't it?

Suvorin didn't give or attend concerts anymore. In a corner of his mind there's still a piano, however—a place to put photos.

How young they all once were. Always with one foot in prison, which even long after Stalin's death could mean exile, a labor camp, the end, plain and simple. A dead man in no time, or at the very least a dying one. And you died slowly. It's better we drink to it than let ourselves be discouraged.

A waiter hurrying by stopped to take his order.

I don't drink anymore.

The waiter hurried off.

Sadly, he said, as he picked a flake of tobacco from the corner of his mouth. I can't anymore. That's how it is. Ever since I could drink alcohol, I drank. You don't think about it, you do it. I'm not exactly what you would call a patriot, not in the political sense, but why not admit that we're more broad-minded about our vices than others, and in every interview I always gave the same answer to the question about our relationship to alcohol in Russia. *Old Russian tradition!* Which they translated as "We're Russians, we drink." They couldn't get enough of the subject. Are Russians drinkers because they're unhappy? Unhappy Communists? Was alcohol good for dealing with hunger pangs? Might that be a reason to go to the West, to avoid becoming an alcoholic? They pulled out all the stops.

I mean really! I'm not a fact sheet. But of course I had one or two lines handy that I developed over the years. Don't trust anyone who doesn't drink! That was one. We felt sorry for people who drank in secret. Most of them didn't live long either. We didn't drink like aristocrats. Plain water glasses were enough for us. To be so close to the flame that a bonfire envelops you, you understand? It shields people from their big country.

I didn't need a thing so long as I was playing piano, but what were you supposed to do with your hands in your free time? Grab a glass! Even today I still have this naked feeling without one.

He looked past my head at something on the wall. The blessing of a long life? I don't know. Just more unfulfillable dreams?

But I wanted to tell you a story. Moscow, Tchaikovsky Hall. An architectural confection. A sliced-open cake. But the acoustics aren't bad. You can be a hero. The air full of spirits. My hands never felt colder. But on the evening of the premiere of my friend Alfred Schnittke's Second Symphony, I was hot. I was burning up, down to my fingertips. Two of my students didn't have tickets for this concert—which wasn't public, no tickets were sold at all. Out of caution. And so they thought up a plan. They were obsessed with getting into that hall. You see, that's how it was. It's not just composers who live off inspiration. They showed up early in the afternoon, dressed like cleaning women. They were let through. In the stairwell they snuck inside a crate that had been slapped together for renovation work. They spent the next four hours in there, until shortly before the concert began.

For the first time he seemed to be aware that I was listening to him. And you, what would you jump in a crate for? But he kept talking, without waiting for an answer, which I wouldn't have been able to give him anyway.

When my wife died a year ago—nothing but a completely senseless and yet just as fatal collision with a city bus—I called one of those two students. Works as a musicologist now. For better or worse, I was obligated to carry out the terms of a will, namely, my wife's wish to be buried in Russian soil. Now, she didn't mean I should ship her body to Moscow. She meant something more poetic. She was homesick. She was like that. Homesick for her native soil. And so I tasked my former student with sending me some Russian soil. Postage paid by recipient, of course. It's heavy stuff.

III

DO YOU REMEMBER?

Vienna is full of Russians, young and old, living and dead, poor and rich. Seems like every time the phone rings there's another one, man or woman, arriving or leaving for good. Everybody has their turn, just as it should be. And for each and every one of them I have a final farewell, a shovelful of Russian soil, a little shovelful, a little spoonful. I've got enough stored up, a whole suitcase full.

Suvorin chuckles to himself. A last little spoonful for myself, too.

He watches with delight as a young woman walks past. You see, he says, that's what they looked like, our girls, only prettier, much prettier, much, much prettier. Each one of us had one or two, and each one was the prettiest. We weren't the kind of folks who have a state funeral waiting for them, but we had a life. They loved us. The prettiest girl of them all loved a man who squinted.

His chuckle rattles with delight.

We married our muses, one after the other, to put them to the test. Of course, you weren't always lucky. More rebuffed marriage proposals than symphonies. More tears than notes. Your head still buzzing from it even today. One guy had saved up for an engagement ring only to have to pawn it after a decree from the father of the bride. I knew a guy who was having trouble writing a love letter. This got around to the woman for whom it was intended, who is meant to have told her husband about it, laughing all the while. One guy fell in love with a fifteen-year-old poet, which aged him in an instant. I saw him again years later in Paris, he attended one of my concerts and came to see me in my dressing room afterward. But it was strange—our first embrace, after such a long time, was like a farewell. His face like snuff tobacco, his voice an octave too low, bags under his eyes, yet he was in high spirits. He was in the company of a woman, an amply endowed German, a good six feet tall and just as wide. She's rich, he informed me, and I congratulated him. We were speaking Russian, she didn't understand us. Very rich! He met her, I learned, on the French Riviera, where she was masquerading as a Baltic baroness. He, on the other hand, had quite truthfully presented himself as a Russian composer, which impressed her. He related to her a few episodes from his life, some true, some fabricated, and promised, after she had confessed to him her love of the violin, to write a violin concerto and dedicate it to her. She was moved almost to tears. He let on, and now at this point he was no longer quite sober, that he had connections in New York, with certain world-class violinists residing there—friends, as he described them. Was this immortality? She dismantled a lobster. She wanted to leave for Leningrad right away. She wanted to shower him with presents, and did so, too. There was no doubting it, a first night together in a Monégasque grand hotel was no longer to be avoided. This was my chance, he whispered in my ear. He did full justice, if he is to be believed, to the superstition that Russians are capable of anything in bed. He wore himself out; then, thinking it was summer and he was living in a villa in Italy rented for him by a devoted patroness, he threw open the windows—and came down with a bad cold. The kettledrum, to use a musical term, looked after him as much as he would allow; he asked for staff paper and pencils. But nothing came to him. The promised concerto for full orchestra and violin never got past the mighty drum roll with which he wanted to begin the piece. He finally managed, on various islands, to write a short first movement, an allegro, for a sonata for violin and piano—so, not much, and as he himself admitted, not exactly a significant work. He also couldn't bring himself to decide whether the second slow movement should be an adagio or an andante, and decided instead to take an extended creative break, which was interrupted by a bout of renal colic. Barely recovered, he presented the woman with a few preliminary notes, scribbled on the margins of restaurant menus, which she then had framed.

The colossal Teuton fell for my friend's fakery with the guilelessness of an idiot, busy as she was finding ways to part with her money—among other things it was her hobby, after she had tired of pearl necklaces and hats, to collect earrings; and, while still in bed, which she never left before noon, she liked to have her composer massage her stomach, which, he said, felt quite revolting, like "spoiled honey."

Is there any explanation for the things people do to themselves? And, if not, is there some method, some means of saving yourself?

I shouldn't talk like this, he apologized, since I'm the one who's worthless. Is it her fault that I'm all washed up as a composer? When she asks if I find her attractive, I have to control myself so I don't get red in the face. And it's hard to believe, but she has a sense of humor, especially when she's been drinking. If I'm too fat for you, or too old, you can have me at half price! There's still that at least!

That she was the one to make the decisions about everything they did went without saying. She taught him manners, dressed him in clothes that suited her taste more than his, taught him to give generous tips, to shave twice a day, and not to spit into his handkerchief at the table. Without a doubt, after many difficult years Zagursky had landed on his feet for once. Zagursky—or as his calling card now presented him, with his full name: Leonid Andreivitch Zagursky—now led the life of a bon vivant, though at this point he did so without enthusiasm and in increasingly unstable, compromised health. Gone was the vitality that at first had led him to believe himself the director of a comedy in which he appeared in the star role, gave cues to the other actors, and made the curtain rise or fall at his whim. Tragedy waited in the wings.

More and more often he asked himself: Why am I doing this?

He couldn't bring himself to admit the truth to her, the whole truth about his complete lack of compositional inspiration—and his fondness for cabbage soup and chamomile tea. When he thought of the hopelessness of his situation, the paltriness of his existence, thought of all the personal as well as professional lies that he spouted out of vanity, but still more out of despair, from morning to night, he could feel icy sweat form on his forehead. The results issued to him by the doctors he consulted (and whom she paid for) were unambiguous. I have it in writing. My demise, my dear old friend, seems inevitable.

I had to laugh. What don't I have in writing.

I complimented the two of them, I didn't want to upset my friend. But I felt sorry for him. A helpless Russian, yet another, who can't leave off trying to impress the world with sheer might. But he couldn't fool me, his old friend. The sun, instead of tempering him, had dried him out. He was drifting toward his end, and seemed to be letting it happen. Reeling with weakness, he clung tight to me—still sweaty and wearing my tailcoat—like a man falling.

I understood it all quite well. Having to like people whom you abhor saps you of strength. As does being at a woman's beck and call. And having to endure opulent champagne dinners every night. And after midnight, when she's dropping a strawberry into her champagne glass, worrying about how you'll manage to stay on your feet.

Zagursky tore at his strong, still jet-black hair. Oh gods of my youth! Oh Samara, city of my childhood! Oh happiness that has left me! No time left to work. There's not even time to rest, to simply sit there and not think about anything.

Once upon a time there was, my friend, I said.

Once upon a time there was everything, he said, life, laughter, good times with women. Gone, gone. He called out names, names of friends. How are they?

They're dying.

And for you, too, Zagursky, a little shovelful, I thought. We won't see each other again, not on this earth.

Do you remember? We all made music, scribbled down notes, played them, alone, together, with each other, over one another, against one another, in private, in public. We fought. It was spring. It rained often, which it rarely does here. Here it simply rains too little. I can't live without rain. I suffocate without rain. He took a few sheets of music that lay on the piano, ran a hand over them, and I saw how he turned away so that I wouldn't catch him fighting back tears. In those days, if you had worked, you earned for yourself the joys of an endless night . . . And today?

For my part, I answered him, I go to sleep after the evening news.

Suvorin signals the waiter and asks for a glass of water. He takes from a bag one, two, three, four, five—five small different-colored pills, a little family, which he beds in the palm of his hand and stares at for a long time. Bright as they are, they won't save me.

IV

WAS THIS THEIR HANDIWORK?

You ask me if I still keep up with my piano playing. I'll tell you, I don't, not anymore, not for many years now, and it's not just the piano I've stopped keeping up with. Life isn't easy. My hands are bored, my heart's worn out, to say nothing about how my legs feel. When I go to the kitchen to make myself some coffee, I forget that I've gone to the kitchen to make myself some coffee. But by that time I'm already standing in the kitchen, which hasn't smelled very pleasant for quite some time now. At my age nothing smells very pleasant anymore. My bed. I'm ashamed to sleep in this bed, but at night I get tired. What am I supposed to do if not lie down in this bed to sleep? It is a joy, a small one, to get out of my clothes, which have the smell on them of long arduous days, of entire weeks. Even if I've made it through the day not in a bad mood, my pants smell of despair, my shirt smells like my socks, like the hallway where the smell starts and then pours out into the other rooms, and the kitchen as well, of course. So long as I'm here there's little use in opening the windows. If the sun is shining, the warm air just pushes the smell back through the window into the apartment. If it's raining, I get to hope that things will be made fresh again. Or I tell myself I do. Rain washes the world clean, that's what they said in the villages where I grew up. Even the old would pour themselves a glass when the sky turned dark and the wind and the rain started in. We were all quiet, because that's how it always was. Everyone listened, even me, even the boys. No one would have dared say a single word.

A holy silence, which I only ever found again in music—later, much later, when I began to love music. I won't say when I began to understand music. Even today I don't think I have any idea what music is. I sit at the piano, I play, I love what I'm playing, but I understand nothing. After midnight, when I'd had enough to drink, I sometimes played like someone who'd been allowed to trick himself into believing he understood what he was doing. I was at my best at these times. I liked to drink. We all liked to drink. All musicians drank. If we wanted to sober up, we couldn't stop drinking. These rare hours, they were what mattered. The hours before sunrise, when I was alone with my hands on the piano and the music that I played. I don't know if I was happy. I was concerned with more important things than being happy. Even today I have no interest in the answer to that question. Sometimes I think the whole of a person's happiness rests on his wanting neither to seek nor to find it. Still happier the person who doesn't make a fuss about it, whether happy or unhappy. Not questioning whatever judgment is imposed upon us. Showing the same equanimity in remembering and in forgetting. I've told myself for a long time, nothing can happen to you, whatever God might do. I hear his angels in the apartment. I hear them listening when I sit at the piano. I hear the quiet of their presence. Maybe that's what I wanted when I played: to make angels sing, to make their invisibility, their silence, ring out. Angels are a good audience, the best a musician can ask for. The young and old women who bathed me as a child believed in all that. None of them played an instrument. When I started playing, they felt guilty. A piano in a village. A child who doesn't sleep. What had they done, where had they gone wrong with this child, who didn't stare up at the sky or into the pots in the kitchen or at the books that were lying around, but at his hands, at how they fluttered when he moved his fingers, how they galloped when they moved? Was this their handiwork? Artists only existed in cheap novels, so easy to pass from hand to hand, wherever you are in the world. That far away from Moscow, artists were a figment of the imagination. The horse that drew the plow was not, nor was poverty, nor the ground in which so little grew. What was supposed to happen? I kept still, if only outwardly so, when in the parlor the old people, the whole family, sat around the table, silent, eyes closed. I did not have to risk much for my pleasure, I stuck my hands in my pants pockets and moved my fingers in secret. I still think of all those people who pray in silence when I think of music. When I listen to music, I still hear the rain in every note. And so, depending on how you look at it, I never really left my village, not in London, not in Paris or Vienna. And I never took my hands out of my pockets. I played like I practiced. Even onstage I had the feeling that what I did, I did in secret. I was at home. I was in my childhood. How long ago that was. Too long to try to trick myself about it now. Nowadays I'll say that, where I'm concerned, playing the piano no longer makes sense. I lack all the necessary strength. The strength of the night, the burning clarity in my head, there only in the deepest exhaustion. Today I'm a smelly old person in a dark apartment, which now that my wife is dead is far too big. I live on a diet of medication, very expensive medication. I don't have a choice. I am old. I am trapped in a body, without hope. Even if I haven't managed to get rid of you, I don't receive visitors anymore. Well, with the exception of a young violinist, who whenever she comes to my door I ask inside, a violinist who despite her youth has had a lot of success all over the world, whose father was a friend of mine and whose mother in her youth was considered one of the most beautiful but also one of the most stubborn women in all of Moldavia, an object of temptation for every one of us. Everything you need to make music on a violin the daughter inherited from her mother, plus her temperament and her beauty, which she considers a nuisance. She's hard on herself, which I like. I don't hold back either. It's not about beating your rivals. And careful, don't burn yourself up before the first note. You're not going for a record! Everything develops slowly. Play the dead like they're your contemporaries, and play your contemporaries like classics. She listens, doe-eyed. The audience isn't in charge, especially not the lords and ladies in the orchestra seats. Don't look at them! And don't let them love you! We speak in our language. I serve tap water. A way of passing the time. I enjoy it, but I feel myself getting tired. I can't keep up the concentration the young thing demands of me for long, and soon I'm no longer even capable of thanking her for the compliments she pays me, and for the gift of a diversion, a change of pace, which she has given me with her excitement for music and her innate recklessness, at least where her conception of the violin and a career without compromises are concerned. I can't even prevent her from taking me in her arms when she says goodbye. This is always embarrassing for me. Doesn't she smell it? Doesn't she see the pile of unwashed dishes in the sink, the dust on the letters that are lying around everywhere? No, she doesn't—or she acts like she doesn't. She wants to save me, to get me back onstage, wants to appear alongside me, the old man and the girl, she says, and laughs. It'd make me happy, she says, I want to. You've still got it, even now. There's no one who plays like you. You'll get yourself back into shape. I trust you. Do it, she begs, do it for me. We'll make it happen. We'll travel together. My God, she's about to burst into tears. Somehow we both keep standing there like that for a while, both ashamed, both helpless, but, we know, lost to each other. It's better if you go now, I say. Well before midnight I'm finished as a human being and fall into bed.

At what would be the right time for making music, I'm snoring. I miss those hours, oh how I miss them! The hours that decided every truth, the hours that were good to me, that brought order to my mind. Brought the requisite disorder, to put it better. Or better still, a kind of higher order. The late Schumann. The Russian alcoholics. Czechs who didn't sleep at night. This time was everything, the time of hyperactive weariness. Even for Sibelius, who tormented himself with his music and with alcohol. Who, driven to despair by loneliness and isolation, listened to the night. No, said Suvorin, with the photograph of his wife on the wall over the table, whatever is played before midnight sounds like nothing. Even in the concerts that I myself played, it sounded like nothing. But who would dare take the risk of allowing a concert to begin after midnight? Even with free admission it wouldn't work. Oh night, sing the poets, and it's not just the romantics among them who are singing. There are good arguments to be made against sobriety. The soul opens up in darkness. It is capricious, as we know. It is an owl. It hides in the light. And, like me, it wants to be alone.

I didn't even notice that she was still standing there. And only now, after these last words, which I had spoken to myself, did she go.

V

HOW LONG DOES AN
INTERMISSION LAST?

I hadn't heard from Suvorin in a long time. Either he'd just stopped picking up the phone or he was lying sick in bed or was in the hospital or, who knows, he was taking the waters in one of the many Lower Austrian spas near Vienna. The other people I asked about him were also concerned—though not overly concerned, I thought. The old gentleman is tough, said one of the waiters at La Gondola. Could be. He seemed like it, anyway: a man with a small, stocky, but powerful build; you could describe him to a child like so: Imagine a good-natured old man, a Russian, with Asiatic facial features inherited from his forebears, the product of generations of different tribes intermingling, a child of the Russian steppe, who grew up far beyond the Urals, propped atop a yak, more resting than riding. Now let's throw in a fiery red sunset, and in the broad expanse of sky a few solitary birds. Nothing about the man suggests the kind of skill that could prove useful when seated at a grand piano. His bones ache. That's why he does everything so slowly, I think, to spare himself pain, pain that even the medication he takes doesn't fully alleviate. He lifts the cup he's drinking from to his lips so cautiously, you might think he no longer knew exactly where his mouth was. He has the pallid skin of a sick man. His eyes tear up, they can't tolerate the light. When he speaks, you don't always know what he's talking about. Seventy years of life can't just vanish into thin air between sentences.

The horrors of history have left their mark on him. How to survive, that was his problem, not how to be happy. So when you ask him questions, expect no answers. There's too much mixed together in there. The best he can do is deliver fragments of a story that lies locked inside his head and has no beginning or end. Still, he does seem very interested in prolonging each conversation. Whoever might speak with him, let them walk out on the tightrope that he balances on without mortal fear.

Please give the old gentleman our best regards, said the waiter on his way out the door to smoke a cigarette, and tell him we hope he gets better soon.

Not to worry. You said it yourself, he's tough!

And he loves the ladies.

Does he?

It's something I've noticed, hope you don't mind my saying so. He took me aside one time to point a woman out to me who had come in and caught his eye. He liked her, he was really captivated by her eyes. He said to me, she looks like an actress named Simone Signoret. Oh, I said, is that so! The name didn't mean anything to me. It's not something I know much about. When I get done working here, I'm too exhausted to want to do much of anything, to go to the movies for example. But the woman he was talking about was my wife.

I congratulated him on his good taste.

You've known the old gentleman a long time?

Not very long, no. I met him quite by accident at a coffee-house and then saw him again at a small, private gathering. All Russians, and all musicians.

So he's one, too?

This reminded me of Frau Szilay, my neighbor, who once said to me that in Vienna you'd get the impression that there were only two kinds of Russians, millionaires and musicians.

He's more than just a musician, really he's something like a legend.

But I don't think the waiter understood what I was trying to get across, that the old gentleman, as he called him, had fallen outside of time. Nowadays people like him only exist in novels. They're a sorry lot. Why should a waiter who lives off tips give such people much more than a second thought?

He nodded toward a picture on the wall, hung between two mirrors, a landscape, amateurish but not without flair, with lots of blue paint for the sky and the blue ocean, and a palm tree so large it could cover an entire town in deep shade. There, you see? You see that little spot there on the right? He likes it especially, the old gentleman, because he thinks he's discovered something there. He's certain—and of course I did him the courtesy of acting as though I were happy about his discovery—that the painter painted a church in that spot, if only in a hinted-at kind of way. The waiter pointed at what Suvorin thought was a church, a church with onion domes. And then he told me, said the waiter, that it must be the Russian Orthodox church in San Remo, where so many Russians had prayed, including, by the way, Maria Alexandrovna, "our empress," as he said his wife, even in Vienna, couldn't stop calling her. He liked the spot with the little church. The Russians always liked everything down there by the sea, he told me. And as for the palms, they were a present from the czar to his wife, who went there to take the cure for her illnesses. It was the czar himself who had them planted, a whole boulevard of them. What did I think of the painting, the old gentleman wanted to know. No idea. It is what it is. It's him who likes it, not me! Whenever he comes here, first thing he does, he always looks at the painting. He stands there, nobody can get by him, and looks. I don't know, maybe he only comes here because of the painting. We don't talk much. Sometimes he drinks a melange, other than that just water.

The waiter wet a hand-rolled cigarette with his tongue and put it in his mouth. His lighter in one hand and the other already on the door handle, he excused himself and was gone.

I regarded the painting for a few minutes more and thought about Suvorin, about what might be going through his head when he looked at it. Was he not looking for something else when he stood there before it, unconcerned, lost to the world around him? Would he soon be pointing something else out to the waiter? Don't you see the face? The face of a woman?

I was still standing there when the waiter came back. You know what, he said as he paused alongside me for a second. If it were up to me, I'd give your friend the painting. I've often thought about it. Just pick it up off the wall and give it to him, make the old gentleman happy. Yeah, he said, and nodded. I'll talk to the boss, sometime when she's in a good mood.

Suvorin, I remember, claimed—and this only because his wife had claimed this—that San Remo had to be an island, a place that transformed people into flowers, flowers into fish, fish into salt. That's how old the island was. Only fairy tales were older.

Will he start speaking to her? By this point he must imagine that she's hidden herself inside this painting. Is he waiting for her to speak?

Oh Suvorin!

Oh San Remo. Oh Leningrad, now St. Petersburg once more. Oh Moscow. Yeltsin was a drinker. The price of food was going up. Rents were going up. The apartments were hard to heat. I thought about leaving the Soviet Union. How hard life had gotten. The wives—mine, too—had knitted sweaters for the cold, socks and scarves. But even still, Richter and Gilels were there.

Alfred was there, Alfred Schnittke, the composer. Akhmatova was there, the poet. "Let silence be the secret sign / Of those among you who, like me, / Are joined in secret marriage." Word had it that Gould would be coming to Moscow for a concert. Who was Gould? At the start the hall was half empty. After intermission, as if by some miracle, there wasn't an empty seat left. They had to leave the doors open, there were suddenly so many people there. And why? At intermission people got on the telephone, everyone hurried to a phone and told those who hadn't come just what they were missing—a sensation, that's what. Now, how long does an intermission last? Fifteen minutes? It was enough to fill the hall to bursting for the second half. Russians! A people like no other. The Poles are mad Catholics, the Russians mad maniacs. When it comes to the appearance of a musical genius, they shell out a month's salary for a ticket or go into debt. This kid from Canada was worth it, the opportunity was there and wouldn't come again, and remarkably enough he even looked like a genius. Thus had life ordained it. Who would have seen genius in someone like me, even if I had been granted the same gifts? I don't say "blessed with," because genius is a fever, a curse, a damnation, we have enough examples of this. Nothing but poor devils, all of them! On good days I was a pianist, on bad days a piano player, and with this I was content. I was never perfect, I take liberties and had difficulties with colleagues who strove for perfection, often even heated, downright uncompromising arguments, back when we were all students still. What I was after was really the opposite of perfection. What is it anyway, perfection? When I played, I was the boy on the staircase who takes it four, five steps at a time. Every performance was a new chance.

I don't know what it was—the memory of a young love, the sound of her voice?—that interrupted this thought and made

Suvorin come to another, to a subject that, speaking with me on other occasions, he had called "the joy of fulfillment." Do you know what qualities you must possess in order to be a good accompanist? That I always liked, accompanying a singer at the piano. There was nothing I liked to do more. When you accompany a singer, you're playing a different instrument.

I see him climb down off his yak, shake the soil off his hands, drink the tea he's brought with him, search for the pouch with his tobacco in it.

What must you possess? You must listen to the consonants in the words being sung, you don't play the vowels. That's the secret. Richter could do it, I got it from him. And his Nina, whom he lived with in a large apartment near me in Moscow, the tiny, delicate soprano Nina Dorliak, I accompanied his Nina on the piano many times myself.

For the second time a mention of Richter from him. And immediately followed up with a grace note in the form of an anecdote, the veracity of which Suvorin insists he can attest to. Richter, as everyone knew, played slowly, sometimes extremely slowly, and where the slowness of his performances was concerned, he refused to be swayed. He was downright notorious for his slow tempi. When such an authority, a man who in his sheer physicality was so enormous, with those enormous paws of his—when such a man played so slowly, it wasn't something you could ignore or write off as a matter of taste. To witness him at the piano was more than just a musical experience, it was a dramatic event. He looked as if he were tormented by a hopeless ignorance. Here was a performer who was searching for the as yet undiscovered, comparable with an archaeologist who senses a find under the ground on which he stands and begins to dig with the lightest of tools, with a brush, maybe, or a small spoon. The man who starts in with a pickax will destroy everything. Bravura destroys everything. Any interest in success, in seeking admiration for his capabilities as a pianist, was completely alien to Richter. Success was finding the trail of a discovery, the hope of finding it. Richter would probably have most preferred it if his name didn't appear next to the composer's on the playbill at all.

But, well, let's put it this way: he took it too far sometimes, especially when he played Schubert. And that was the case on the evening a friend of mine told me about, who was also a good friend of Richter's. After the concert, as they had agreed, he had gone back to his dressing room, not a journey to be taken lightly. When has any of these big personalities like Richter ever been satisfied with their performance after a concert? Well, Richter wanted to know, did you approve?

This was the very question my friend feared. In all honesty, he had not at all approved of Richter's performance that evening, he had found the slowness pathetic, at times even stultifying. Richter had pushed the slowness to the furthest limits, and beyond. You could say it was his version of religiosity, because for Richter there was nothing more holy than slowness, for slowness he would risk everything. This deserved admiration, but that evening it had also, at the same time, triggered an anxious restlessness in our mutual friend.

So you didn't approve, Richter asked.

I didn't want to upset him, my friend told me, not just then, after such a strength-sapping concert. He had trouble, my friend said, finding the right words; he just stood there in front of Richter, embarrassed, squirming, stammering, hemming and hawing. He started sweating. It happens, you know, when you don't want to lie but you also, out of understandable consideration, don't want to come out with the truth.

And how did Richter, who naturally could sense my friend's

dissatisfaction, react? He seemed just as dejected himself. He was quite vulnerable, even if, looking at him, you wouldn't have guessed it.

I know, Richter said, I know, and I'm sorry! You're right, of course you're right, I didn't play the Schubert slowly enough.

He said it like someone who had sinned.

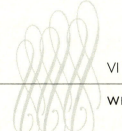

VI

WHAT HAD I DONE?

They called him Padre Piano, a joking reference to Padre Pio, subject of many paintings and statues and deeply revered by the Italians, especially those in the poor South.

They didn't look alike, of course. Nor was there anything holy, or even kindly, about Suvorin, try as you might to find such qualities. It was simply that in his public appearances he had the habit, after the final chord had rung out, of folding his hands on his chest, pausing for a moment—his eyes closed— and then letting them sink into his lap.

What did it mean? Was it even supposed to mean something? No one knew. Had anyone ever asked him about it? I would, provided I could ever get him on the phone again. He hardly ever picked up. He slept a lot. Others, too, whom I asked about him, had neither seen nor spoken to him in a long time.

Suvorin was, despite his love of drinking, a sober man, and thus had he appeared before his audiences all over the world. Unlike others, he wasn't one to strike a pose onstage, neither that of a gladiator wrestling a beast nor that of the lover oppressed by melancholy, which so easily suggests itself during slow movements. Completely foreign to him as well was the idea of attacking the thing he served with the air of a man of suffering. Neither his face nor anything else in his carriage would have gone along with it. For him, music, when he performed it, was work—anything but the everyday kind, true, but still work. Depending on the level of alcohol in his blood, he could work up a sweat as he played just like a worker on the clock, and with a man like him, throughout the many years of his career, you wouldn't have been wrong to think so. It was work, however, that was directed at something more than just music, and even he didn't always know how it could be mastered. You could play it all flawlessly, with the pedal alive, with bravura, passion, with the highest level of prowess. There were and are enough good piano players, after all. What it came down to, along with other things—the right attack, the right tempo, the silence, yes, the silence even in fortissimo—was never to insert yourself into the music with arrogance or the authority of a virtuoso, never to damage its secret. Don't wave any flags, as he put it, neither the Russian nor the Soviet nor any other.

Once—after a concert in Leningrad, I think, it was 1972 and I had played Bartók—a lady came into my dressing room. Now of course, it was like it always was after concerts, pure pandemonium, but this lady plowed her way through everyone. There she stood, right in front of me, staring at me. It's all a question of distance, and it made me uncomfortable how close she was. That gesture, she said, and pointed to my hands. I had no idea what she was talking about. It wasn't the Russian that was spoken in Leningrad. And I wasn't in the mood to want to know. Estonia? A Pole who spoke Russian? I asked her what she meant, what gesture? You folded your hands. You prayed. She was serious. It was clear that my concert had given her not a musical experience, but a religious one. Plus, you could smell it, she must have been wearing a ton of perfume. Me? Prayed? Is that so? I had been sweating, I was thirsty. Plus, where were my cigarettes? Not a good time to listen to compliments. I'm not a preacher. And music doesn't preach either. What the hell was the point of all this? She tried to touch my hands. Not to shake my hand to say thank you, no. To grab hold of them, to touch them like you touch something that isn't of this world. I excused myself. I was soaking wet. What had I done? I'll find out if I can. I know what my hands are doing when they're working, when they're on the keys. But after that? I don't know and am accountable to no one for this ignorance. But I couldn't get it out of my head. Naturally I was interested.

And I, too, was interested. What did I have to lose? I liked the poor man. Though he was no longer very healthy, I still thought he had it in him to fly into a rage, and to live through it, too. Either that or he would act as if he were lost in thought, far away from his past as a working piano player. He had lived too long in exile, his friends were elsewhere or already dead. He had no students left.

And so I asked him, as we sat together in La Gondola—he with a glass of tap water, which the waiter placed before him straightaway along with a pitcher, I with a glass of red wine.

This gesture, what was it about?

Look, he said, and was silent for a long while. I wanted, I think—and if only I could have gotten my wish—after the last chord had rung out, I wanted to be invisible. The fact that I closed my eyes would make you suspect that I was at least trying to be. If I can't see anything, I thought, others can't see anything either. That old child's game, which you probably know yourself. I wanted to hide. And why? Simply put, because I hate applause. What a stupid business, this applauding! Please, I couldn't stand it! Not as somebody up on the stage, which thank God is over with now, but not afterward either, as a listener in the audience, never. The final note, it hasn't even completely faded yet—and immediately you get screaming, noise, people shouting bravo. Not a moment of quiet, not even half a second. What ignorant people! What barbarians! No last reverberation, no lingering in that last echo, no trepidation, wonder, not a hint of abandon in those who had been listening. I actually did pray, every time, that they would be unable to move. Please, you people down there, be quiet! Keep quiet! Stay seated and be quiet. Stand up, leave, do what you like with the music I've played, just don't make a racket. What kind of people are they who, after a sonata by Schubert, the late one in B minor for example, completed two months before his death, break out into cheers? I sensed that everything I had admired, everything I had wanted, the meaning I had given my life, was all over and done with. There was nothing left. The gods are dead! Even today, even now, it weighs on my heart to think of it.

Suvorin ran his hands through his white but still full shock of hair and shook his head. That's what it was, you see, that this gesture was meant to say. My hands on my lips were a plea not to provoke me, not to force me—since what else was I supposed to do—to take a bow, to smile, to play an encore amid that unabating din, not that, too. My God, I thought to myself, what is this? Do I have to listen to this? And if you're not lucky they even press flowers into your hands. Then you have to stand there with them, it's a joke. They've understood nothing, they don't know how wrong they are. Gould was right to quit early. The guy was just thirty-two! But he had had enough and he threw in the towel. Good kid, and he had a sense of humor, too. That he did, you have to hand it to him. While I . . . coward that I was . . . I got angry, kept at it, and went off to have a drink.

It seemed to amuse Suvorin, the coward he was meant to have been. With a smile, he invited me to join him in his amusement. Maybe the woman, it occurred to him, the woman back then, maybe she wasn't as stupid a person as I thought. I should apologize to her if she's still alive. He raised his glass. Which I hereby do. Then he spoke about how the audience treats musicians like prisoners, that it tries to milk them for all they're worth, which he considered an imposition. It was all just a cheat, nothing but a cheat. What was I supposed to do then, if not let my hands sink into my lap? Disappointed every time, furious at my own helplessness. I had prayed for an offering, time and time again. But to become one myself? No.

Suvorin took my glass, the glass with the red wine, in his hand, held it against the light. I felt sorry for him. How I envied the poets, he said, and placed the glass back on the table, and still envy them. All those who write books. There's a—I don't know how to put it—there's a warmth to it, there's dignity, a profound truthfulness. And those guys were taking a risk, too. Every verse was one step closer to the prison camp. Just think of young Brodsky, who on top of that was a Jew! Suvorin poured himself more water, switched suddenly to Russian, speaking more to himself than to me. Although I didn't understand a word, it was probably poetry, verses spoken from memory. Even though he wasn't actually declaiming, there was something solemn about it. Here sat a dispossessed old Russian, whom his doctors had forbidden just about every pleasure, for whom they had prescribed gymnastics sessions and, in his eyes an even worse imposition, had recommended going swimming at a pool—here he sat and granted himself a memory of the Leningrad of his youth, of that everlasting thing which poets create, verses of a poetry rich with dark colors, dangerously beautiful and, the way he spoke it, itself music.

It lasted until the old man found his way back to the table at which he sat and turned his attention back to me and his own thoughts. Look, he said, reading a poem, reading a story or a novel, it isn't a social event. Somebody sits there, just him, alone with himself and a book, and reads. And sometimes, right, he pauses, and puts it aside, still open to the page he was on, in order to think about a sentence, a certain passage, a particular phrase, one that reveals the beauty of the language to him. Everything can bring everything in connection with everything else. He thinks of a child, a woman, a friend, thinks of a day in his life, of the life of someone else who is dead, in prison, banished somewhere far away. He remembers the light of an afternoon, a cloud in the sky, maybe one in the shape of a woman's breast or bottom, a walk, horses standing in a paddock in the cold rain. He has time. There's a lot of thinking in poems.

VII

A CITY ON THE WATER?

I was on my way to my wine shop when I saw Suvorin come out of a supermarket and head toward me. He was in the best of moods. I haven't told you the rest of my story. Do you have time?

Since I settled in Vienna, I can't remember a single day when I was ever in a hurry. And to meet Suvorin on the street, this man who hid himself away, felt to me like pure good fortune.

He headed off toward—where else—the nearby La Gondola, where once we sat down he ordered milk, a large glass of warm milk, "but no foam," he called after the waiter.

I ordered—it was early in the day—an espresso, lit a cigarette, and leaned back. He had quite evidently recovered since our last meeting. Either that or he was full of renewed vigor from a good night's sleep, which had perked him up and would keep him in good form till early afternoon.

It turned out he'd bought himself a pair of swim trunks. Plus dozens of chocolate bars, on sale. Did you know that you can buy swim trunks at the supermarket these days?

The other day at Tchibo, which is a store that sells coffee, I bought a vacuum cleaner!

He rummaged at one of the two plastic bags and brought out the swimsuit. It's nice, I think! It's got the colors of the Italian flag. Here, look!

No foam, said the waiter as he placed Suvorin's glass of milk in front of him. And for you, sir, an espresso!

The colors of the Italian flag? Why those? I asked him.

There's a city down there in Italy that my wife could never stop gushing about, she'd never seen it but always wanted to visit.

I guessed Naples.

So close to a fire-breathing volcano? Out of the question! No! Venice?

A city on the water? She'd be scared of getting seasick.

But what about Leningrad?

A city that is made up of islands, right, over a hundred islands.

I didn't know that. Over a hundred?

So you didn't know, it's not important. Here's something else you don't know. Or you do know it, doesn't matter. Leningrad, if you wanted to count them, has more bridges than Venice.

I conceded defeat. So she couldn't have lived in Leningrad either.

No. Impossible. You see, my friend, not everything we love is bearable. Suvorin seemed amused by his own joke. Next guess, he said, keep going, what's left?

I could have said Rome, but it struck me as too boring. I gave up.

San Remo! His face lit up. San Remo, when the flowers there are blooming. She had read about it somewhere once and fallen in love with the idea of taking a trip down there. And it wouldn't have been too distant a possibility, leaving from Vienna. He looked at me. Of course you know all about that, I suppose, no? For you in the West travel wasn't a problem.

His confession made me feel embarrassed, and the question, too. Well, sure, I said, not really. The one time I was there I didn't find the city interesting enough to even want to spend the night.

He folded up the swimsuit like you might fold up a map and tucked it back in the plastic bag. Maybe, I thought, it was all a way of getting him to go to the swimming pool at some point, like his doctor had recommended.

By the way, Suvorin asked, what was it we were talking about the last time we were here?

I could remember every word he'd said. How impolite the audience was to torment you with applause. And how you envied people who write books.

Right, said Suvorin. I was fed up. I didn't know what to do anymore, where to turn, what would become of me. It was hard to endure. After every concert I had to walk around for two hours to calm myself down.

I knew the feeling. Often I've thought, if I could only fall asleep while I walked, I'd be saved!

And then I got thirsty and needed company. You know what I mean, booze and tobacco! What's better than setting aside whatever worries you have. And no women with us at the table, no one anywhere nearby to talk about alcoholism and scold us and say we were going to poison ourselves. Suvorin sighed. If only.

I didn't really know how to read him, neither his sighs nor his laughs. Which was suffering, which was shtick? Or had he developed the art—perhaps essential for a person like him to survive—of concealing from every interlocutor precisely what could be used to lure him into a trap?

Naturally a few people were concerned, and after a while they started to worry about me—or started making jokes. One of them suggested I should have flyers distributed among the audience with the notice: *Applause absolutely prohibited! Audience response unwelcome!* Or go ahead and make the announcement myself, the equivalent of what Schoenberg, famously, had rigidly implemented in Vienna before the war. Not a bad idea, but why rehash old news? Then came old Schwarzberg, who as it happens also ended up in Vienna, a violinist who never had any objections whatsoever to applause—to the contrary, she enjoyed it, let the waves wash right over her—applause, she said, relaxes the muscles. She had the best solution yet. "With your talent, Yurka, I suggest you just give the good people a real fright. After all, everybody knows you're a born joker. You play the concert and then, before you have to acknowledge the applause, clutch at your heart and fall off your stool, right onto the floor— preferably without injuring yourself of course! *Did anyone hear a shot? Is it a heart attack?* I bet the hall goes quiet instantly. The only risk is that it might get you talked about, get you in the headlines, and, if you're unlucky, make you famous! And famous people in this country, as you know, are even applauded as they're put into their graves."

Suvorin liked the idea. They carry him off into the wings. A doctor is summoned. They fear the worst. Had something like that ever been done before?

But there was a problem. It wasn't right to make a joke of dying. His conscience forbade it. More than that, his mother's memory forbade it. How could he, who had made death a laughing matter, stand before her grave? What deprivation she had taken upon herself so that he could live his dream, to play piano and to study with a teacher in Moscow in order to be able to play better and better and, one day, make the leap to the stage. Her face always grew very serious when she imagined her son's life and spoke to him about it, his life after she herself would be dead. These talks invariably boiled down to a single piece of advice, which ran: Pray, don't dictate. She believed herself to be in the right. It was advice not just for him, her only child, who, surprising everyone in his immediate and extended family, had become a musician; she gave the same advice to everyone who was in need of protection and understanding in the world. Less and less lucid in her final years, she would repeat it again and again, but by then it was only dismissed as the talk of a demented woman.

She had an easy death. She herself had blown out the last candle that burned by her deathbed.

I had colleagues who advised me to see a neurologist. To their minds, anyone who had purchased a concert ticket had thereby gained the right to make a spectacle of himself—had paid for it, so to speak. They didn't understand all the fuss I made about it. Even my little daughter, who knew a hypnotist, got involved. She's the type who believes in that kind of thing, even today. Spiritualism! Miraculous icons! It's an old Russian sickness, you know, saints, wandering monks, hocus-pocus. And vodka of course. Thank God I had a good, sensible wife. Always positive. Whenever anyone told her she should snap me out of it, get me to see reason before I hurt my career, she would laugh and answer, "He's not going to change, not a chance. He is what he is, an enfant terrible!" In Russian: *On svoloch'!* Which you can also translate, please pardon the language, as "He's an asshole!"

Suvorin laughed as his wife might have laughed.

That's how we lived. We were happy. God bless her soul!

He went silent, as he always did whenever he was reminded of the loss he had suffered with the death of his wife. He took a sip of milk, wiped his mouth, scratched his stubble for a moment. How fearless she was, how clever, how witty. She took it for granted that I'd drawn the wrong kind of attention because of my attitude toward the official Soviet music apparatus, and was therefore no more surprised than I when one day a functionary from the State Repertory Committee stood at the door, sent there with orders to talk some sense into me—in the friendliest way possible, of course—on account of my behavior. A man who spurns his fellow man's joy in applauding spurns his fellow man. Art, Comrade Suvorin, belongs to the people. Did he not love his people? Was it not clear to him that in his capacity as a practicing musician he was meant to be in the people's service, to stand with all his heart in the service of love for his people? What is the highest calling of all those who make art if not to make that which is dear to the common man, that which touches the heart, that which summons solidarity with the simple people, the working masses? Did he not want to fortify the people with optimism, with the authentic, the true, the—in musical terms—melodious? To shield them with all his strength from all that is false, all that is corrupt, all that corrodes the spirit of our society, that is to say, from anti-Soviet, revisionist, counterrevolutionary ideas?

He didn't stutter, oh no, he had what he was saying down pat, it was more than well oiled, it oozed. And again and again as he spoke, he would smooth down his tie. I waited—both of us, my wife and I, waited patiently, very patiently, for the finale. And it came, in sound compositional form, with short, powerful chords. He spoke of the Great Friendship, but also of the Great Error; of the great magnanimity of those who ruled, their indulgence of certain sins—but said that it wouldn't be undangerous for deviants, as he called them, to take things too far.

He sat there at our table, legs crossed, satisfied with himself; asked, since he was a smoker, for an ashtray and, since he immediately started to cough, for something to drink. He acted like we were all going to strike a bargain: in return for the plainly manifest friendliness with which he meant to impress us, I should have the good sense to admit my mistakes, or, in official bureaucratic Russian, to "rid myself of political errors."

Not right away, though, not here and now, that's not what he was asking, not at all.

I could already see myself, if not arrested—not that—then nevertheless pressed into service of the collective, into serving the people, detained and put in the usual straitjacket for pianists. I wouldn't be the first, and certainly not the last, to get off with what was of course, relatively speaking, the light punishment of accompanying silent movies at the piano.

I wasn't mistaken. They would order me to repent. But the first order was just a simple, apparently harmless question. Surely you love the movies, don't you?

Whether it was the banalities that he'd memorized and sat there spouting off word for word, or the one little glass—albeit filled to the brim—of vodka that I had permitted myself in the kitchen while my wife took his coat from him and led him into our living room—I just felt like punishing him. Here was a person who came around looking to strike fear into another person, in this case me. Besides that, I knew that I had an ally in my wife, and I knew that I didn't want to disappoint her.

You speak, sir, with an old voice. As if from the grave. Old voice, old thoughts, old, very old habits, and bad ones, too. Aren't we about the same age? No? Unlike you, who know what profession I practice, I don't know anything about you. I see you wear a wedding ring. All the same, that doesn't tell me how happy your marriage is. You act friendly, but are you? Do your parents have any other children? Do you take more after your mother or your father? And your siblings, if you have any, are they like you? Assiduous, ambitious, never drawing attention to themselves by talking back? Like I said, I know nothing about you, less than nothing. What kind of success are you striving for? You want to make the crooked straight? Why exactly are you wearing a tie? And—how imaginative, how profound—a red one at that? How many like me are left on your list for today? How many poets, professors, composers? Why all this effort? Why repeat history, why reenact so many past crimes?

When you leave this apartment, I said, someone could easily mistake you for harmless, a man out taking a stroll. Which you most assuredly are not. But what—and above all, who—are you when you go knocking on strangers' doors? When you're doing it, do you feel good about what you are? With what life has made of you? I had him, I could tell. He was helpless before me. Now, whatever I did, I just couldn't give up; I also couldn't react to my wife gently kicking my shin under the table. Onward, then. New questions, more questions, spoken as soon as they came to me. What dreams did you have as a young boy? When you and I still wore short pants and wool socks, even in the summer?

I looked him straight in the eye as I said all this. We, you and I, could have been friends. Friends who wanted to fall in love with girls. Who swore to be true to each other, like a boy and girl would. Barely a year later we would have gotten drunk together. We would have been free, young, and careless. And happy, without knowing what happiness would feel like later on. Isn't that still what it's all about, being happy? All right, good, let's get to work on being it, then. I spoke without passion, in a soft, calm tone, like a river shimmering in the sun, which invites you to look at it, not to jump in. I had no idea that it was a profession, being an optimist. But that too is old, finding the others, the doubters, the difficult, the unknowing, the misled, to seek them out, to visit them in their homes—to pursue them. What does your conscience say about it? Have you ever thought about it? Aren't you afraid?

I leaned forward. He would have understood me even if I had whispered it. When you look at me—as you're doing now—

you don't see me, you only see what you stand to gain. Can you ever switch it off? What do you see when you look at your wife? Come now, no weaknesses? No time for them either? Even Beethoven had some.

A shame that under these circumstances it wasn't possible to fortify myself with another glass. But even still, my strength held out long enough to bring his punishment to an end. I ask myself how long it takes for someone like you to transform, to go from being a man who'd only just been lying under a blanket, asleep, rolled up like an embryo in his mother's belly, maybe dreaming whatever it is he dreamed, and on waking up felt the warmth of a female body next to his—how long does it take to transform into a man who barely gives himself time to eat his breakfast in peace, say a kind word to his wife, tell her he loves her, who's in such a hurry to save the world, or at least the most valuable part of it—his own—and to pursue his career as a good comrade serving authority? Is a cold shower all it takes? A shave? What are you exactly, a functionary, an ideologue, a pesky little—

Another kick in the shin! And this one hurt. And got me to shut up.

I can still hear my wife, after she had listened to all the accusations brought against me, and then my diatribe, and after that his and my silence, saying to the man, "I'll buy him a saxophone, that way he can make music and do it only for himself."

And again Suvorin laughed and took his time laughing. A man of great, profound sadness. Who laughs.

Nowhere else do the authorities have such crushing power as ours do, said Suvorin. They sent movers to take the "Red October" out of the apartment, that was the brand of piano I had, it was on loan from the state conservatory. Okay, comrade, fine by me. What a farce! Did he really think he was hurting me? The "Estonia," a mass-produced Soviet Steinway copy that I got moved into the apartment a week later as a makeshift replacement—it belonged to a friend of mine, a private individual, it was actually his Bechstein I'd had my eyes on—did the job well enough, ultimately even better than I thought it would, but what an ungainly thing it was, its nickname was "the tank," and rightly so. In every "House of Culture" in every tiny town in the nation, no matter how remote, sat one of these indestructible things, but how could you play the fleeting tones of a Debussy on it, or give voice to Schubert's tumbling sadness? So, on that front at least, things seemed less than promising. I wouldn't have dared set foot on any stage abroad with that beast. Not a trace of refinement in its tone. Its action was stiff, which I had problems with in the beginning, but what choice did I have? I just had to experiment, get used to it, break it in. But even still, something was missing, and the most crucial thing at that. Well, so it went. A copy doesn't always have to be a bad thing, necessarily, but what you can't copy is what we call "the soul of the instrument." Can't be done, not with "the tank."

Suvorin sat up straighter. But then, wait till you hear this! Are you listening? Laughing had brought his good mood back. I was sitting with my wife one evening at a beer hall, which wasn't exactly a habit of ours, but one of my students had found out that they poured good Czech beer there, the best beer in the world, he claimed. And so we went. He was right, the beer was in fact excellent, really, although I usually don't touch beer. And besides that, too, everything was just right. Pleasant, ordinary people, all very natural and friendly, and even though there were people talking at every table, the room was filled with a soft, pleasant stillness. We talked about—what else—my distress in front of crowds, the insolence of crowds, which I had encountered yet again a few days earlier, we were playing Tchaikovsky, his Trio op. 50, I had put up with it, gritting my teeth, even though I wanted to scream, or, even better, to start throwing punches. Of course we also talked about everything else we were worried about, our future, our lives, our children's lives, and what kind of opportunity still existed given the latest completely arbitrary cultural-political rulings and resolutions. At that point a man sitting with his beer at the table next to ours, without being at all intrusive, joined in on our conversation. He spoke the words that were to change my life: "Play," he said, "what no one likes, then you won't get any applause."

Suvorin clapped his open palm to his forehead. What had the man said? Play what no one likes? Find a different audience, one that doesn't get dressed up, one without the least propensity for any manner of exaggerated ceremoniousness? I was, I'll admit, stunned to have encountered so unexpectedly a person of such thoroughly pragmatic makeup, someone who didn't spend a lot of time hung up on all sorts of compunctions about this or that.

Suvorin was silent for a long time before he started talking again.

And then there was something else, something very personal that was troubling me. For some time, you see, I had been noticing a few things about myself that I didn't like, I didn't like them one bit, a tendency toward pettiness, a nasty outlook, dejection. I was acting aggrieved. I pitied myself. I was, what can I say, disappointed in myself, very disappointed. Old and used up already!

Suvorin looked right at me. Play what no one likes! Didn't that mean, in fact, set off in search of people who suffer as you do? Good Lord! If that wasn't worth a try! I think I grabbed my wife by the shoulders and gave her a kiss. Don't wage war—struggle! To hell with people who behave as though they were the owners of this music and, worse than that, the arbiters of morality and respectability.

His eyes danced.

I had a new card up my sleeve. No more would I stand around in stagnant, stinking water; I swam for the open sea. Beethoven, Brahms, Schumann, I could play them whenever I wanted, for myself, my wife and friends, and playing chamber music with colleagues, which I actually did, there's simply nothing better. But my interest in a public career, in front of an audience that had shown time and time again that it would never learn, melted then like snow in spring!

He felt the change as soon as his choice had been made.

I'll tell you something—in my head I had already packed my bags.

Your bags?

Off to San Remo!

Well of course, where else!

It was funny. Not even ten minutes ago I had been thinking the exact same thing. Suvorin, playing piano in a hotel bar, one of the old grand hotels naturally, and in so doing granting one of his wife's deepest wishes.

I would have made a decent bar pianist. What do you think?

So what went wrong, then?

When my wife sees a suitcase, she gets homesick, that's what.

Oh, this laugh, when he laughed. It didn't just do him good, and I could see it did, but me as well, and he never missed an opportunity to let it out. At the same time, he did the surly grump routine better than anyone, it was masterful.

Besides, even if she denied it, she was jealous. You see, she'd read up on it, there weren't just blooming flowers there, but also young women in bloom; and also of course those who were a bit more mature, wealthy, very wealthy ladies, with or without pet dogs. There wasn't a single woman on God's green earth whom she didn't see as dangerous. But to accuse me of anything, or make a scene, no. She never raised her voice, and she didn't cry either. All she did, if she suspected something, was to get conspicuously quiet. She, who liked to be so boisterous, who hummed songs to herself, who could marvel at falling snow as only a child could, and that in wintry Leningrad, lost all interest in everything, including in herself. How quiet she could be— and how beautiful, the way she moved.

In another of our conversations he had once called her "the woman who would never die."

I began to feel ill at ease. I could tell how deeply the memory of his wife affected Suvorin. He would probably have preferred to be in other company than mine just then, at a table with good, old friends, lost in thought. He would have liked, I could tell by looking at him, to have kept on talking about her, little things, all so precious now that he was the only one of them still living.

Back then, he said, there wasn't a single one of my fellow students at the conservatory in Moscow who hadn't courted her. And for a long time it looked like an open race, everyone was vying for her favor—even if I was the one who gave himself the longest odds; I didn't think there was a chance that she could fall in love with me, of all people. When I saw her she was shy. When she saw me, she looked away. She was too good for just one of us, on that we all agreed, when we were sitting together and had had a bit to drink. Too great a gift for one man alone! When, many months later—in my whole life there was never a time that felt longer than those weeks and weeks—it happened that there was a chance meeting between us, she didn't want to go back home, never again, she said, never again alone. And then she gave me a kiss. How do you grasp such a thing? Why me? How come? What did she see in me? Who was I then? Or was I someone I didn't know? Did she want to help me find him? I was still counting on the worst when I proposed to her.

In the meantime La Gondola had filled up with lunchtime customers. Suvorin was distracted for a moment when one of the waiters went past our table carrying a tray bearing different plates of pasta. The food looked good, and Suvorin breathed in its aroma. The moment for remembering the life now behind him was gone.

She didn't trust me for a second, my little bangtail, and with good reason. Why lie? But was it that bad? No! Who would we have been, my friends and I, if we hadn't put on a big show and tried to outdo one another with our foolish boasting? His conscience, he said, was clear. We were decent guys, he said.

Suvorin sighed like someone who hadn't merely packed his bags back then but had actually stepped off the train in San Remo, who had made his dream a reality, who over the course of many summers and just as many winters had earned his money as a pianist in the hotel bars down there, good money, who against his will had gotten used to champagne, had spoiled his wife and enjoyed himself and recalled with wistfulness the loveliness of certain chambermaids.

They stayed in Leningrad.

When he was discouraged, his wife would tell him of San Remo, of blooming flowers and—so she did have some sense of humor—of young women in bloom.

I started fresh, more and more I played only for young people, for contemporaries, played the most current, the most difficult, the most undesired, the forbidden. Shredded and distressing sounds, called forth by tone clusters, tritones, percussive attacks, irregular rhythms, microtonality. All fodder for my "tank."

Music without melody, music of obliteration, of moments drawn out and distorted. I ordered myself to play pieces that met with resistance. Who was going to clap their hands off now? What I—and a few others with me—was doing was naturally an act of disobedience—the attempt, as we jokingly called it, to make a proper meal out of ketchup and horseradish. I was a pianist trained in the Soviet Union, that is, a pianist patronized by the state, who was placing himself in the way of the official cultural politics of our country. You should know that the path from state-sanctioned artist to enemy of the state was a short one back then. All it took was a signature on a certain piece of paper, a call, a summons. Informants were at the concerts. You had to be prepared for anything, day and night. But afraid? No! Afraid for my children, maybe, but I left that to my clever, brave wife; if it came down to it, she would be able to explain to them what was happening better than I could. As far as I was concerned, it was like I'd been reborn. I was alive again. I could breathe again, I could live. I heard whistling and catcalls, not applause. The auditorium doors slamming shut. What I unfortunately never experienced at a concert was a riot, a proper brawl, with people fainting all around me. What a shame! But still, to have insults thrown at me instead of flowers wasn't too bad either.

Suvorin beamed, his whole face lit up. Saved at the last minute!

At some point Suvorin even saw the man from the beer hall again, out in the audience. There he sat in the same clothes he had been wearing at the bar, the suit that didn't fit right, the shirt that was darned and wrinkled and missing buttons; he sat there and listened to something he couldn't have been used to hearing, at least that's what I assumed. When I took a bow after the concert, the bow was directed at him more than anyone else. He'd gotten through it! Now I was the one who felt like applauding. If I were a peasant, I remember thinking, I would have showered him with chickens for roasting, with butter and fresh milk from the countryside, for something had changed for me not only musically but also, how to put this, but also as a person. The sentiment against me made me into a peaceful, gentle person. In this state I could have met every condition necessary for playing Bach. Interesting, isn't it? I did play him, of course. I can't imagine a pianist who would give up Bach. He's part of what counts as hygiene in our profession, he's indispensable. It's like brushing your teeth. It's calisthenics for the ears.

Suvorin shook with laughter as he recalled a comment that he'd once heard from the mouth of a colleague, who no more shared his enthusiasm for Bach than did that French writer especially renowned for her quick wit who is credited with originating the bon mot in question: he, Bach, was nothing more than an "inspired sewing machine."

We both laughed.

Bach, he said, was a person's best ally in the battle against despair, against the thought of how immeasurably great one's solitude is in the endlessness of the universe.

I wouldn't have thought that Bach could become ever more important to me the older I got. To be sure, so far as I could help it, I only ever played him in small churches in the countryside; I went wandering with him, so to speak, from village to village. Bach, after all, is a composer with whose music you associate concentration, silence, reflection. Boisterous ovations, you would think, would really be sort of intuitively prohibited. The people who came to listen shared my way of thinking. The applause was as it should be, heartfelt, polite, it came from within. We were a congregation, myself and those who had listened to the music.

All of a sudden Suvorin became pensive, turned his head

this way and that, as if he were listening for the notes he had played back then. What a beautiful language German can be when you don't scream it. *Lauschen!* What a word! It's got everything: the attention, you're completely absorbed; the intimacy, you're alone with what you're hearing. It's how you listen to the birds, to the breath of a sleeping child. But of course there I was, I lived in the capital, and there, on the battlefield, so to speak, I concentrated completely on the most difficult, the out-and-out modern, and the audience, the people who for a long time now I hadn't wanted anything to do with, didn't put up with it for long. Communism has its bourgeoisie, too, of course, and still does today, no less indolent or self-satisfied than they were in their time in Paris or St. Petersburg. Still, it shouldn't be forgotten, without them we wouldn't have the scandals, those brilliant explosions in art, the cleansing storms. I was there when one of them came down with the force of a hurricane during one of our concerts. A soprano, in good voice, held in her hands as she sang not sheet music, but a coffee grinder—and she kept grinding away. That got their blood boiling, those fine ladies and gentlemen. And then, well, that was that. Little by little the rows emptied and once abandoned were quickly filled, as the newspapers wrote of the incident, with young people, with students, with dissidents, with loners, poets and writers, with people who'd had enough of the stagnation in their country and, more than that, had the courage to come out of hiding.

Suvorin smiled at his own excitement, how it was still exhilarating, even now. Our catacomb concerts, as we called them, were at any rate a complete success. Life suddenly seemed bright and thrilling to me again.

The fingers that he had been warming on his glass of milk for as long as it was still warm now took on a life of their own, like little birds, which, this I'd been waiting for, got him thinking back to our first conversation. Of course I couldn't, and I don't know why not, break the habit of making the gesture, he said. You know what I mean, the gesture of folding my hands together at the end of a concert, which earned me that silly nickname, but now it took on a completely different, a new meaning. This was a gesture of gratitude. I played, without making any concessions, for the curious, and I was grateful. And relieved—and how! Once I had finished playing, I let my hands fall in my lap out of sheer relief.

And this he did, he acted it out.

But wasn't it the case, I asked, that the people still ended up rewarding your performance at the piano with applause? Surely they weren't all quiet.

He looked indignant. Of course not. I even took a bow, which I had always disliked doing. Actually I only ever hinted at doing it, I wanted off that stage as quickly as possible. No one could ever have talked me into doing an encore. But here! What a difference there was. There was nothing for me to get angry about. The applause was honest, it owed nothing to convention, it had the same, I would say, the same measured force that my hands had to use on the keys so as not to lose control while playing such difficult music. Believe me, sometimes the music those guys wrote was enough to make you dizzy. It makes me think of the cuckoo in a story by Chekhov, where it's said that its call sounds like it "kept reckoning someone's years and losing count and beginning again."

But, he admitted, stepping offstage with a bow also had its advantages. It provided me with information about my spinal column, especially the condition of my intervertebral discs, which were always giving me trouble. If your back hurt when you took a bow, the next day you called the masseur, who straightened you out again. And you've always got to inspect your shoes, when your head's down and your eyes are open. Maybe it's time to finally get rid of this or that pair, even if they're still comfortable?

You didn't experience those years, said Suvorin, but the people didn't just clap because they were having fun. It was also a demonstration, this was opposition, protest, resistance! Which of course, I admit, made it even more fun. Whoever clapped was demanding the freedom of art. Or better yet: demanding freedom, plain and simple! You were going to the barricades, even if it was only a concert hall. It was beautiful mayhem.

VIII

WOULD YOU COME WITH ME?

Whenever people ask me, and how often in my life have they asked me this, if there's a connection between music and alcohol, I recommend Beethoven. Don't listen, as many would have you believe, to the drunken Russians, listen to Beethoven. Listen long and listen closely. Beethoven begins with the end and then he can't stop.

Of course no one understands this. But that's fine. It's fine just to say something right. What's right is puzzling enough, after all.

It was an unusually sunny and warm day for mid-October, a Sunday, the streets almost deserted. Only Suvorin was out and about.

He had spent the morning in the attempt to find the half-dozen pills he was prescribed to take daily, which he had mislaid. What a hardship it had become, really it was shameful, not being able to find your way around inside your own home, within your own four walls; and of course these days he didn't live as modestly as all that, it wasn't just four, it was five times four walls altogether, plus a long hallway lined with bookcases from end to end. He could hardly find anything anymore.

I can't even find the words to describe to you the full extent of the misery I'm on the verge of drowning in.

He was exaggerating, I was sure of it. You could tell by looking at him. He made a comedy of his distress, with him as the leading actor. It amused him.

I happened to notice just then how neatly his nails were cut.

I'm in the most awful situation. I can't find anything anymore, not my glasses, not my keys, not the letters that, some of them, I haven't even opened. Of course the most frustrating thing is the recipes, which, when I finally do find them, are so smeared with butter or coffee stains that they're barely legible and therefore useless.

Even if, as I assumed, some of this was overstated, the question of how he spent his days was moot. It was quite certain that he was making his way through a maze, that of his apartment, that of the city, that of his wandering course through a life that would have driven so many others to surrender, if not to suicide.

And in dreams, too, he wandered, dreams, of this I am certain, that were not kind to him. The years leapt after him, the bad ones were in a hurry, the good ones less so. What revealed itself to him then—when, more and more soaked in his own perspiration—he fell asleep, was the misery of a life brought low, illuminated before the eyes of a crowd of people the size of an orchestra. They all spoke Russian, were gaping at him, ripping posters from the walls with his name on them. Old Schwarzberg wore a Sisters of Mercy uniform as she carried him off the stage. She was in the best of moods as she warmed up some vegetable soup for him, as if this were the most normal thing you could do in a dressing room. Suddenly ten years younger, she took her violin from its case and, with the full weight of her even then royally corpulent body, plopped herself down onto the stomach of a waiting doctor, for whom this was an honor. Then she was gone. The doctor as well. The dressing room, when I died, was empty. With this feeling I woke up.

Would you come with me? There's bound to be at least one pharmacy open.

On the other hand, it then occurred to him, I occasionally find certain things that I wasn't even looking for, a little volume of poems, that book on Bartók, a certain piano arrangement, an Italian language textbook. When I got to San Remo I wanted to be able to open my mouth, after all. But of course, as you know, nothing came of it, neither the one thing nor the other. San Remo remained a pretty sound, a name, and as for the book, with its tables and lessons, well, to be honest, it doesn't look like it's seen a lot of use. I've cracked it open a few times, paged through it and said *amore* like other people say *amen*, but then I closed it again and set it aside; I could never bring myself to do anything more. Sometimes, though, when I'm looking around like this, I find money I thought I'd lost, stray bills in books and in pockets.

I know what you mean, I said. Happens to me, too.

Except then I just put the money away somewhere else, where it gets lost again. All it takes is a handful of dirty laundry that I mean to take to the laundromat, and already the money is gone, tucked away into something else.

Not a bad idea for a comedy.

Do you believe, he asked me, in something like animal magnetism? Does something like that exist?

Since I like to believe in something that eludes logic, the domineering power of our reason, I nodded. Yes, it exists. I've always believed that things seek me out. Things wait. Things have souls.

That, and more than that, he said. The soul, he said, isn't something you can hold in your hand. Is a sound that I produce on the piano a thing? What is a melody?

I was struck by an entirely different thought. Now I was the one asking him something. Does this happen to you sometimes? There's a state of great inner calm, in which past and future trade places? The past lies before me like a still-uncharted landscape, while the future falls farther behind me with every step I take.

It ends in despair, was his answer, if you don't fall asleep first.

Though all the pharmacy doors were closed to him, there was one that stood open, I myself had stepped through it an hour earlier and, so as not to bother a woman praying at the altar, lowered myself onto one of the pews in the very back: the door to St. Josef zu Margareten, the small church in which, as indicated by a plaque to the right of the entrance, the body of Franz Schubert had received final commendation.

But Suvorin was in no mood for worship. Whatever there might be to believe in, he'd forgotten it.

And so he just stood there, looking left and right across the intersection, unable to decide whether to take a step in one direction or the other. An old Russian in Vienna, a dry drinker, a dry pianist, as he had once called himself, the no-longer-distant end of his earthly life in view. This matter seemed not to concern him at the moment, however. He was still alive, if no longer quite in sync with life; he felt the heat of the day warm his bones and travel through his body down to his feet. It was like that when he still drank, too.

No agitation, says my doctor, he said, and no alcohol, not a drop, which, because I have to listen to it again and again, gets me so agitated that I have to have a smoke, although of course I'm not supposed to do that either. He turned to me. You don't happen to have any cigarettes on you?

I handed him my pack. And went ahead and lit one myself.

It's not a sight I like to see: a man who smokes a cigarette with a guilty conscience and lets it burn down to the filter. He didn't throw it away either—he spit it out.

What about you? Do you drink?

After sunset and only in company, which to my taste shouldn't mean more than two or three people—friends stopping by.

And do you ever really cut loose and overdo it sometimes?

I got off the strong stuff a long time ago. That's behind me now, thank God. Red wine, two, three glasses. The difference in age between us isn't all that big.

Two, three glasses, he repeated, his hand in the shadow of the bottle. That's what I see when I close my eyes. I look east. I see the faces of my friends. I see nights growing lighter. I see, this is also true, a madman.

Down the whole length of Schönbrunner Straße nothing is moving, not even a curtain, not even a single face behind a curtain.

He still couldn't decide whether he should walk a little while longer, with me or alone, or go back to his apartment and turn it upside down again in search of his medicine.

Do you know the disappointment you feel at a fork in the road, at not being able to go in both directions at once? I'm not a philosopher. I don't understand it. It's the same with drinking. Every decision is the wrong decision.

IX

WHO KNOWS WHO IT IS YOU'RE

TALKING TO?

What is it, perfection?

A carpenter knows. The boards are flush.

The soccer player who kicks an unstoppable penalty—he knows it, too.

A sharpshooter hits the bull's-eye, and does it five out of five times.

A bank robber has the perfect plan, but it all goes wrong. Every architect alive could also tell you a story like that. The blueprints are perfect, things get botched during construction.

For a dancer, the only perfect leap would be one that lifted him to such a height over the boards that no one in the audience could believe it, nor he himself either, back in his dressing room after the performance was over. He even stuck the landing effortlessly, lifted his arms, and then closed his eyes. Before taking his bow, he put his hand on his heart. Was it really he who danced? Did he dance that he dreamed? He doesn't dare be happy.

A man I once had a conversation with in the restaurant car of an ICE train—a math professor, as it turned out—was certain: water. There was nothing, he said, that was more perfect than water in motion. For his wife, who was with him, this wasn't poetic, wasn't romantic enough. She envisioned the water of a mountain stream. With a radiant blue sky above, the mathematician teased, then pulled her toward him and kissed her.

That hat looks perfect on you, I heard the saleswoman say to a customer.

We, Suvorin and I, were talking about it on the phone. One of the rare occasions he bothered to pick up.

Do you remember? The boy you once described yourself as being, who took the stairs three, four at a time.

I didn't say where the boy on the stairs was headed, upstairs to his room or downstairs to the street, whether he was in a hurry or just in a good mood, a bit carried away, a bit reckless. If he was unlucky, he'd break his foot. And the girl he had a date with would be mad at him for the rest of his life for standing her up.

So should he be careful?

Better yet, she's waiting for him in his room, and he can't get there fast enough. That way she can console the unlucky boy, whom the happiness of love has made incautious, console him with all she's got. This is love, she'll think, but only after she takes him to the hospital and sees him lying in his sickbed, a cast on his foot. All on account of her. On the way home things are going through her head that have to do with love, or at least with emotions. Nothing but nonsense. She mistrusts any sentiment that she can laugh at. When she feels something, she wants to plumb its depths, but at the same time is afraid of the depths, since everything deep she associates with darkness. On the other hand, there's still the hope that she just doesn't know enough yet about such things. Who knows, maybe somewhere down below, in the darkness of deep emotion, there's a door that could open onto an inner courtyard, a place like the gardens of paradise the Renaissance painters used to paint—quiet, bright, joyful. When she arrives at the door to her apartment, her head is spinning like crazy. Yet again, she knows nothing.

That's how it was with Suvorin. In just a few sentences, spoken very slowly, he makes children grow, a boy becomes a man, a girl a woman, and the two of them enter into something that bears all the usual shortcomings of a love affair.

Good luck, he calls after them. And: Hope the foot gets better.

The old man, I think, is once more taking pleasure in refusing me an answer to my questions. And, as always, I'm half amused, half infuriated when I take note of this.

He holds out his hands and wants to know if I notice anything about them.

They're strong, they don't tremble. Not necessarily the hands of a virtuoso.

Well?

What am I supposed to say?

The fingernails on my left hand grow faster than those on my right. Funny, right? When I noticed it, I took a look at my toenails.

And?

Nothing.

These were the kinds of jokes with which Suvorin entertained himself—himself more than others. He made no allowances. Did you know that Bowles, when he was still making music, once composed a piece for trumpet, cello, and two birds? And notated it all on the door of a toilet stall in some hotel, I think in Tangier, where he used to hang around. To his credit, it's said that he didn't try to do anything when he saw the maid come around and wipe it off.

Did he at least take a photograph of the score beforehand?

Of course not!

I saw it in his face. How could someone he took for an intelligent guy ask such a question?

Suvorin played. He was a piano player. He would have liked

to have had the time that he had now when he started playing. Enough time, which to him now meant time for stories. Lots of people wanted him to tell them things, in conversation, in interrogations. Thus it was wise to give yourself time when answering, just as it could be wise when entering a house to go in through the back door. With facts you don't know your way around as well as you do with allusions. The best response to obstinacy is agreement. Age has its advantages in that respect. We're only halfway living in the present, and those who have a future, our children, should be the ones to concern themselves with it.

Suvorin plays with his answers like children play with putty. Who knows who it is you're talking to.

There was thus no sense in trying to approach him head-on. What do you think it is, perfection, for a practicing musician? Is it important? Is it possible? How valuable is it? Does it make everything good or does it destroy the best, the most precious?

There's no difference between that young woman and me. She knows nothing. I know nothing. We all know nothing. No one knows anything. What perfection is? Whoever knows it, knows nothing. Yet it's the crucial question, crucial probably for everything that has to do with making music. That's why it's urgent. The question exists, but the answer does not. Having a sense of humor doesn't help either, unfortunately. You have to decide. When I taught at the conservatory in Kharkiv, I had to do it every day. There were students, young, talented people, whom I could either accept into my class or refuse. How do you decide? Well, there were a few criteria. Anyone who started in with lots of drama was out of luck. The same with all those who clearly cared too much about trying to impress me. I'm not a king. I don't rule, I react. I can tell when someone overestimates himself. If a lion tamer overestimates himself with a pack of lions, he gets pounced on, torn to bits. A tightrope walker should take care he doesn't get too full of himself up there. The good blacksmith speaks with the iron. A poet said it quite nicely in a poem: But when the angel appears, be alone, so that you might receive him.

And that's how I received the young people. Liszt? Oh no. Chopin? Please don't. It doesn't absolutely have to be Brahms either. Instead I handed everyone who signed up for an audition a small, nice bit of music by Schubert, in and of itself insignificant, seemingly completely harmless, easy to sight-read, his Kupelwieser Waltz, a sheet of notebook paper, nothing more, as far as I know it doesn't even have an opus number. Happily enough, it only takes about a minute and a half to play the waltz, which might seem unjust to some, but in my opinion it presents a reliable method; besides that, those one and a half minutes are an advantage not to be underestimated, given the crush of students waiting outside the door. Anyway, no one, I've found, ever needs more time to show everything they can do right or, indeed, wrong; nor do I need more time to make whatever discoveries need to be made about a student's musical intelligence. Which brings us to that question about perfection. But don't get your hopes up that you'll get a valid answer, from me or from anybody else. What could it be?

I wasn't expecting this. He had talked himself into a frenzy. Only a bit more, and only because I mentioned the little waltz. The mortal sin with Schubert is trying to play him perfectly. It makes no sense, none at all. You have to do the opposite, you have to—how should I put it—it's more like you have to play him clumsily, a little tipsily, or better yet, drunkenly, helplessly, shakily, almost ignorantly, with an understanding, an inkling at least of an era in which people, even if they did cut loose and dance, still felt shame, still blushed. With Schubert there's a lot of keeping silent. Everything is directed inward. I knew enough people who got quieter and quieter when they drank; Schubert did it when he composed. This was someone who had no idea who he was, or at least he didn't know that he was endowed with great genius. I don't want to hear about immortality. You have to have it in your heart, and in your wrist.

I heard him snort.

One more thing, but then enough for today. Often, when I wake up, in the morning or in the afternoon after a little nap, and then especially, I have the feeling of having been dead, a strong, not even unpleasant feeling. That's how you should play Schubert.

I could still hear him saying all this when I arrived at the Hotel Imperial and made myself comfortable in the lobby, helped myself to the local and international newspapers lying around and ordered a melange. It was a few minutes before I stumbled upon an interesting report in *The New York Times*, an article about a theater director who was putting on a production of *A Streetcar Named Desire* by Tennessee Williams and was in the process of looking for an actor to play the male lead, the role of Stanley Kowalski. And what did I read there? He didn't have the applicants act out a scene, no, didn't have them recite any lines either, nothing that a director normally does before he casts a role. He called the young men in, one after the other, and asked them to say one word, one word only—well, okay, two to be precise: "Hey, Stella!"

Naturally, like you and I, every one of them remembered the film, famous because of leading actor Marlon Brando's portrayal of Stanley Kowalski, and remembered how he calls out for his girl, how often, how impatiently, more despairing with every breath.

To get the job with a scream. In every respect that was the truth about the lives of so many unemployed actors, who struggled along as waiters, as delivery boys, as boxers if they had the guts, and waited for a chance, that one chance that changes everything—and so of course every candidate had been rehearsing his audition in his head over and over again. And now this!

How do you get warmed up under the stipulation that you're only allowed to open your mouth once? How do you work up the tension you could have used to allow the character to develop, if that isn't what you're being asked to do?

In any case the director didn't look like someone you could argue with, as was made quite clear to one of the candidates, who was sure he could handle what was expected of him, who had even brought a friend, also in the business, to be his scene partner. He, like most of the actors auditioning, had internalized every detail of Brando's performance, had trained his muscles, lifted weights, done push-ups. He had cut holes in his unwashed T-shirt; this article of clothing promised him strength and confidence. He was going to nail it, this was supposed to be his moment. And now it all boiled down to the bare minimum, to nothing. "It would be better if you left," the director's assistant suggested to the scene partner. It was said kindly, but was unmistakably an order to vacate the premises. Everything within the young man rebelled against the whoring that was clearly just business as usual in this profession. Shouldn't he just pack it all in and keep hauling boxes around or washing glasses? His scream, when it came, sounded appropriately sad and dispirited.

Another had brought a sandwich with him, since he figured the audition could take a while. And he bit into it, more out of nervousness than calculation, and with his mouth full shouted the line he was asked to say. That's how it went, he told the newspaperman, and I figured, well, I screwed up again.

Stella! Hey, Stella!!

Suvorin will be angry when I tell him this. His minute and a half has clearly been beat.

X

WHERE DID HE STILL BELONG?

From the year 2012 on, Suvorin had been alone. His two children, a daughter and a son, both grown, lived elsewhere. How close they are, he can't say. It seems to him that, when apart—that is, together in thought—they have a greater sense of each other than when they're actually present together during their visits. That they exist changes nothing. After the death of his beloved wife he couldn't be consoled, not for two long years. The days when he can't find his way around weigh on him, every single hour. His own life doesn't belong to him anymore. Others' lives don't interest him. He seeks relief, wants to protect himself without being bound to well-meaning people.

He wants to transform himself, to become someone who no longer has to live. This is what he thinks about. He doesn't arrive at a conclusion.

He falls into a depression. Whatever he sets out to do, he can't carry through, and what he does manage to do, he can't control. He wants to maintain a shared life that no longer exists, a life with a dead woman. How dead are the dead? Those things of hers that are still in the apartment no longer breathe.

What can a man count on once his life has collapsed, what talent, what aspect of his character? What is it that not even his own death could take from him? How about *resolve*? It's not a pretty word, not a resonant word that a man who's been touched by death and waits silently in the dark behind unopened curtains can place his trust in, but it's one with substance: *resolve!*

In the wild years in Moscow he and his friends had wanted to struggle like heroes whose creed was "Think radically and act with resolve, no matter the circumstances," just as though they were under the watchful eye of God. They would have had a hard time forgiving themselves for moral laxity, and their wives would have as well.

In Karlovy Vary, he remembered, he and his wife had gone looking for the stone statue of Beethoven, and then finally found him in one of the little parks. For a long time they stood standing in front of him. Everything within him had driven him forward. Nothing had seemed capable of holding him back—not madness, not weather, and not Goethe, whom he was meant to have encountered here. Impressive, how he bares his forehead to the storm, his coat blown open. Well sure, Suvorin's wife had said, better this than living in New York.

Suvorin pounds the piano with his fists, then he pounds the keys, like a man who's lost all control and started a fight with himself, if not an all-out brawl. Hard, wild, riven music, which, though improvised, seems familiar. It pounds against the walls of the world. Only music that hasn't been composed yet can be made to explode.

He doesn't like the kind of relief that this produces, no, but it fills the emptiness within him. In the space within him, something necessary emerges. This is enough.

Does death make love greater? Operas make this claim. Dreamers as well, who have an entirely uncomplicated approach to the custom of embracing death—his dark angels. So long as health cooperates, it's nothing but theory. The final sigh isn't a cough. It resounds.

Such are the shadow plays of romanticism, which weren't to Suvorin's taste. He couldn't even bring himself to play romantic piano music romantically. He had no interest in staking a grand claim for himself on this terrain. In poems, what stood on the page were beautiful gifts, magic; this he accepted. But when it came to what held people together, it was about reliability. He took a sober view of things.

Well, it was over and done with now. The project of growing old together was ruined.

And so he went, as soon as the practical matters had been taken care of—finding a gravesite; winding his way between the different authorities, embassies, and consulates; standing in line and waiting here and there; finally the funeral itself, now lawful thanks to all the papers requested and validated with signatures and stamps—so he went to church, a Russian Orthodox church, which he had hardly ever visited and which he entered without crossing himself.

He was very quiet. He was weak.

A man came down the aisle with a toolbox in hand, actually a priest, he had apparently been busy with some task that, neatly enough, had something to do with the order of things in the world.

They looked at each other.

Here I am, a little man in need of help, said Suvorin. Those were his actual words. Thus had they occurred to him. Brief and polite, very much to his taste. Yes, the little man! A brother he had found there, a new friend.

In order to improve his German after his arrival in Vienna, and because he planned to do so with novels written in the German language, he sought out secondhand bookshops, browsed around for reading material suitable to his purposes, and decided on a book with the title *Little Man, What Now?*, a novel by an author named Hans Fallada, which he got at a good price. He said this like someone asked to submit a statement for the record.

He was neither trembling nor crying. It occurred to him, though, that he had no feeling left in his hands, in both hands. It seemed to him then as if he would never again be able to move them as he once could.

No one should get too close to another man's pain, said the priest, which was exactly what Suvorin thought as well. He was fed up with the pity, the advice, suggestions about what would do him good. He declined invitations to houses in the country. He was looking for a way out, not company. What was he supposed to do out there? What could have healed him? Was he supposed to sit there picking his nose while everyone said prayers for him? Hand the wife of his host a bouquet of self-picked wildflowers so as not to be thought of as the person she took him for, a gruff, perpetually ill-rested pessimist? Better to take a spade and turn over the soil, dig up the whole earth from one end to the other!

Where did he still belong?

To the priest, the man was a stranger, a Russian like him, a man from yet another of the many tribes of the vast empire that Russia had been.

They spoke to each other in their own language.

The little man no longer resembled the artist who, not so long ago, had filled the concert halls of Europe, Wigmore Hall in London, the Parisian Salle Pleyel, and not just those, his hands folded together at the end. His teeth were bad. His movements were stiff. But he wanted to live, otherwise he wouldn't have turned up here.

Did the little man think of suicide? It's not something you give interviews about. There is a record, however, of a comment he made, years before the accident that killed his wife. Suicide? No. That would mean murdering the woman who gave birth to me.

He was thinking then of something quite different, of something as useful as a toolbox. Clearly in churches there was work to do, for laypeople as well. He'd thought it up on the way there. Showing up every day at a set time. He would perform whatever task he was given. He wouldn't make any demands. He wouldn't think himself too good for anything. He would have to get up, wash, get dressed. He would go the whole way on foot. Behind him he would have locked the door to an apartment that it would require strength to return to. Where would he find that strength?

The priest lived in a house of strength. And he had the good fortune of being reminded of this, again and again, by the people who took refuge in his church, which bolstered his strength in turn. Not the regular worshippers, present at all occasions, his congregation, the many familiar faces, but someone like this man, who said only that he was a Russian, that he had lost his wife, that the children were out of the house. What now?

The little man spoke to the priest and was able to make himself understood; he entered the service of St. Nicholas, bought himself an alarm clock, and showed up for work on time, every day except Sundays and feast days, every day for a full two years. His belief that he wasn't allowed to get sick, and the regularity of his work, rigidly adhering to the staff schedule, sheltered him. They were duties that he took seriously. They brought him closer not to God, but rather to the still-distant day on which, healed, he could release himself. It would be easy enough to find another sorrow-burdened person to dust the icons and refill the oil in the lamps.

Sometimes, when he had finished his work for the day, the church was filled with song, with the bright and somber voices of the choir that held its rehearsals there. Otherwise it was quiet, as it had been quiet after his performances in the churches filled with his countrymen. All their hands were still.

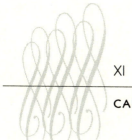

XI

CAN YOU HEAR ME?

Only early on in the time we knew each other did I make the mistake of thinking that when Suvorin asked questions he was interested in answers. These were questions like "And how about you? Tell me! What's your connection to music?"

Maybe it was age, the state of his health, his absentmindedness, whether put on or actual, that made him view as highly incidental everything having to do with the world or the people in it. I, whose company, I think, he enjoyed, was no exception in this. He liked me, was happy to see me, but was too weary to be curious, his future too short and me too young to have a chance against the harm that communism and alcohol had worked on his life. I am a man, he told me, who is dying too slowly. I've had what I wanted to have and survived what could have killed me.

I could see it, looking at him. What interest was it of his, what was to come?

As waiters served customers and greeted customers, vanished into the kitchen and reappeared, loaded down with plates, Suvorin sat there, indifferent, his eyes trained on something unknown.

I said nothing.

And what about you? Tell me! What's your connection to music?

No, I wouldn't fall for it again. I simply waited until he had recovered or picked up the thread of what he wanted to say, this or that verse by Pushkin, a comment on a marriage, the harm that healthy food can do.

Pardon?

I hadn't misheard.

Water and bread and no reading any newspapers, he said, and laughed. And one forbidden cigarette a day.

A moment passed, a very long moment, before he added: To accept what we think.

He placed both hands on the table, straightening his posture, and afterward moved his fingers in a particular way, as if he were testing their mobility—a habit that, I assumed, no longer reminded him of the black and white keys of a grand piano, but nevertheless remained the kind of gesture you would expect only from a pianist (and, of course, a magician, before he baffles his audience with a flying card trick).

I, too, was baffled. How much can go on inside a mind? How scattered can it be, how, if you want to call it that, poetic—for, after a silence, without any reference to anything that we had been discussing, he said: To see the light above the ocean and, above this light, those who have left us.

I'm not sure I understood everything that came out of his mouth on this or other occasions. Some of what he said made it sound as though we would never see each other again. It was a premonition.

It didn't stop with lost thoughts, wandering thoughts. Maybe it's true after all, he said thoughtfully, that in the end you increasingly come to resemble those you were fighting against. Or you're always, from the very beginning, your own worst enemy. He stayed in pursuit of this thought, his face rigid, unmoving. You don't run into life, he said, you spend an entire life running after it. And then they take from you even the most precious thing, sadness.

Scattered, truly.

One of the waiters, when he came by, put his hand on Suvorin's shoulder. They were kind to him, all of them. They liked him. They intervened only when he desired it. Once, when one of them set a flower on the table in a little matching vase, he made a face expressing such dissatisfaction that the waiter apologized and immediately took it away.

And you, he said to me, what about you, tell me!

Maybe, I thought, I should do it, write him a letter, I should write Suvorin a letter like a child would. It might be of interest to him.

Or it might not! Other than bills, does he even get any mail these days? His mailbox, which he can barely bring himself to empty, must be full of them, as overstuffed as the trash cans in the courtyard. No doubt if he even still checks his mail it's only by chance (when he happens to find the key!). And if we're going to talk about bills, there are others to settle, the one with God, for example, who isn't exactly one of his favorites. The pitiful affairs of man are one thing, but the trick of proving yourself worthy of His attention is quite another, and Suvorin hadn't always managed it. Still, the Beneficent One, the Exalted One had provided. He had cast His sunlight into the face of that bus driver with such accuracy, right at the moment when he was making a turn, had showered his eyes so suddenly with light, before he had a chance to shield them with his hand—and on top of that had seen to it that a rider distracted him at the same time by knocking on the glass divider—that for a moment he wasn't just distracted, he was plain blind. Suvorin's wife had taken the brunt of it, she was dead. And all she wanted was to run across the street to pick up a *Gugelhupf* to have with her coffee, they always had them at her bakery on Thursdays, the ones with the raisins.

He'll have to pull himself together, says a Viennese woman who lives in the building, life goes on, after all. But if you ask me, he should take a little more care with his appearance, don't you think? He's had milk in his beard for who knows how long. Someone needs to straighten his collar. I saw the Russians after the war, they were different. It's hard for the poor man. But am I supposed to get worked up about it?

It happened quickly, at least there was that, said the police officer. This was after he had taken his hat off, pinned it between his upper arm and his body, and drawn himself upright. He should have kept the news he had to deliver to himself. Once someone in military uniform shows up, that means the worst has come, Suvorin's father had taught him that, having learned it firsthand, and he, his son, had never forgotten it. Nothing would be the same as it was before, there were the bombs, the soldiers marching past, whole armies, snow covered the world and covered the pain.

I'm sorry, said the officer. But as soon as we've learned something about the exact sequence of events . . .

No, nothing, the door was already shut, locked, bolted, twice, top and bottom. There was no mistaking it, the widower wanted to make certain that he could be alone.

Suvorin turned off the radio (which was playing a quiz show just then, not exactly challenging, but entertaining; he never missed an episode if he could help it), closed the curtains, saw spots moving suddenly in the material, yellow spots with a light green shimmering at the edges, lots of them, a veritable rain of fluttering, twirling, tiny bolts of lightning, which also danced above the carpet, along the wall above the wood of a shelf. At any other time someone could have found joy in this play of light, now it took an effort to bear up against it. He pressed the backs of his hands into his eyes, waited for the effect, which didn't set in as he'd hoped, not right away. When the fluttering flickering finally calmed down, the spots of color became streaks, blurred, and dissolved; when he could again see normally, he threw the curtains wide once more and opened the window. Below he saw the policeman crossing the street, without looking left or right.

Thanks, he murmured as he walked past his grand piano and closed the lid, thanks very much.

He went looking for the soil, just to be sure. There wasn't much left.

A traffic accident, not uncommon, statistically. We read about one every day in the newspaper, or don't read about it, it doesn't concern us.

I know the route, it takes the bus past a cemetery on its way to the airport, and if at that moment I'm in my seat and not busy looking for my plane ticket, I always see a group of mourners outside, flowers in their hands, there to bid farewell to a father, a mother, a husband, a wife, a child, a close friend. I spare myself the pain of opening my heart to this tableau. I know my heart, know how it struggles with everything, how easily it can be overwhelmed. If we're not stuck in traffic outside the gate, it helps to take deep breaths, for at least as long as it takes until I myself am standing among the mourners (and watching the bus driving past) or, with heavy heart, am myself the one mourned. But wait! Why am I writing *with heavy heart*? Does it have to be like this? Is there no other way, no easier way, of bidding farewell? To put it differently: Are there more or less intelligent ways of mourning? And of course a man facing the end could also ask himself whether there might be things he didn't do quite right over the course of his life if he expects the ones closest to him to cry their eyes out once he's vanished from their midst. Adieu, ample life! Bring on the merriment of my final days. Go ahead and shovel eternity into the earth with me. And when you're finished, get back on the bus; and don't forget your ticket.

The apparent obscures the fundamental, life obscures death. The earth doesn't have me yet, and it won't till after what will hopefully be a soft landing at my destination.

There's no point in protesting, whether against God or against the belief in Him. The best you can do is resign yourself to the insight that only despair can bring you, that death, too, is nothing more than an unfathomably irrevocable folly of fate.

Did Suvorin ever really believe in God, and if so, which God, from which tradition? The one with the beard or the one without? I don't know, I never asked. Maybe my lack of curiosity robbed me of an inventive answer. I can't help but think of the interview he once gave a French newspaper. "God, no, I'm not, no! I'm the man who invented blue milk!" he's meant to have exclaimed to the journalist, after the latter had taken him for an atheist. "In a purely musical sense, of course."

What's it like when you're alone? How alone is alone? Are you bored? Or is your mind fully occupied with the struggle against loneliness? Is loneliness visible? Is it a disease, curable, incurable? Are you hurting a lonely person when you ask him how he is? Can you ask him about dreams, dreams that he has or would like to have, dreams he's afraid to dream?

Could a letter consisting only of questions make him reply? A letter like the letters children write?

Why is God invisible? I want to be invisible, too, then I could get away with anything, I could do or not do whatever I wanted, then watch what happened afterward. But I'd be afraid, too. Is God ever afraid? My parents don't like it when I talk like this. My sister thinks I'm dumb whenever I get started. What a bunch of junk, she says. Who wants to be invisible? Of course she doesn't get it, she does everything she can to get noticed. She doesn't just want to be visible, it's even worse, she wants to be unmissable. If you'd like to be invisible, she says, good for you, I've got nothing against it, it means I'd finally get you out of my hair.

The retainer she has to wear drives her nuts. She's suffering, which isn't just her own private business, because I'm suffering from it, too, we all are, actually, the whole family. She doesn't talk about anything else, which is bad enough, plus she also doesn't listen to me whenever I try to help her. I can be reasonable when I want to be, I've told her over and over again to just keep her mouth shut, then nobody will see the retainer. Just keep your mouth shut, I say. That's how things are between us.

Can you hear me? Are you still reading? Please write me back.

But no, I knew he wouldn't write back. He had once, if in a different context, let slip the following remark: Letters? No, I don't write any, for the simple reason that I want to spare myself the torment of having to wait for replies. I had even written this comment down in a notebook—for potential future use.

You don't know me, I don't know you, which seems fair to me. I think it's important that neither of us is trying to take advantage of the other. I'm not saying we're equals, for God's sake. If we were, then it would be possible to think that you would write me a letter, which is completely out of the question, on the one hand because, like I said, you don't know me, and on the other because I assume you've got all the answers to all my questions. I'm sure of it. I trust you. To write a letter like this to somebody else, one of my friends for example, or one of my teachers, would be completely pointless. It would lead to misunderstandings, not to answers or a conversation, which, if I might permit myself to dream, would of course be the nicest thing of all, a conversation with you.

What do you dream of? I think I already asked you that. I'm repeating myself, sorry—you see, I don't want to bore you. I know what it's like to be bored. My family are pros at it.

So? I'll write my address with lots of hope (which I don't have!), it's probably best I write it in all capitals. You see, I live in Vienna, too, so the letter I'll be so longingly waiting for, of that I can assure you, shouldn't have to travel longer than two weeks to get from the part of the city where you live to the one where I live.

Already I've asked you so many questions and I've totally forgotten the most important one. It's almost a habit with me by now, at least my mother says it is; my forgetfulness is going to drive her insane, she says, but I don't believe that for a second. She's too nice for that. She loves me. She and my father have a subscription to the opera. She likes to go, she says she does, but I'm not entirely sure I buy it. I think the only reason she goes to the opera is because beforehand, in the morning, she gets to go to the hairdresser, which she really takes her time with, it's almost a ritual for her. Afterward she doesn't just look like she's just gone to the hairdresser, she smells like it, too. So of course when she goes to the opera she doesn't want to be invisible. Actually everybody except for me smells like the hairdresser's, there ought to be a law against that. It doesn't get anyone anywhere. It also doesn't have anything to do with any opera that I know.

If you're about to take a break, to scratch your head or to think for a second or something like that, please don't ask me, even if it's just in your head, whether operas have anything to do with anything. That would definitely be the hardest question you could ask right now. If my teacher asked me a question like that, I'd say, to make him mad: They have something to do with music. Clever, right? And not even wrong, I don't think. You can do without a lot, you can even do without the audience, but not the music, not in opera. It works like a magnet, which I know because I have one. I play with it and can't explain it, not really. Can a magnet pull apart a drop of water? No. That would be something, if you could use a magnet to lift water into the air, a creek like the one behind our house, redirect it like it was on a leash. I only mention this because music must also have something to do with water, I feel like. Notes are like waves that rise and then break. With music you can swim way out, let yourself drift. I left myself a reminder: to understand music, look at the water! The Danube, the Black Sea, the Mediterranean, the big ocean that goes all the way to America. Search the water for a coastline, an end, an end to the world.

I've just got this feeling like I have to get off my ass! Just looking at the ocean in my atlas or taking a quick walk won't get me anywhere, I know. I'd like to travel. I haven't seen any of it yet. I would consider it an honor if you could help.

Nah am Wasser gebaut, I'm sure you're familiar with the expression. Built close to the water. It means "weepy." "So pretty you could cry," that's what my mother says when they're singing an aria onstage and I feel her hand on mine, because maybe she's forgotten that I'm only her son. It's just a shame that her actions don't match her words. I've never seen her crying or even having to fight back tears. I've cried, though, more than enough times. I can't help it. I get choked up trying not to get choked up. Doesn't work, not a chance. My mother, though, who knows how she does it, who knows what's on her mind. My guess, and I'm sure I'm not too far off the mark, is that she's not thinking of the Danube or the ocean, but rather the nasty effects that tears would have on her face. Her makeup, her mascara! What if it all got smeared when she cried! Anyway, she gets through it all still high and dry, and on the way home she even has the comment handy that I cry enough for the both of us. I guess you have to hand it to her, she's never at a loss for words. Not even an hour after everybody onstage is dead, she can be cheery again. What I'm supposed to think of such behavior, I don't know. Actually, I'm disappointed, and once, in the tram that was taking us home after a performance, I even told her so—I mean, I hinted at it. They're just stories, she said, which hopefully you aren't taking too much to heart. She gave me a hug, lovingly. Of course not, I said, so she wouldn't get worked up. I mean, after all, I don't want to end up being the kind of person whose parents remember him as problematic. Anyway, they talk about me enough already and get worried even if all I'm doing is staring at a wall. I can do it for half a day without getting bored. I don't move, I don't think at all, I'm not awake and I'm not sleeping either. It's like at the opera when everything inside me fills up with music. Those times, too, it's only with a lot of effort that I come to my senses again. Really, though, it's the exact opposite, I'm actually making a great effort trying not to have to come to my senses again at all. For my parents it's weird to see me in this state. Abnormal behavior, my father calls it, he says there are going to be consequences if I don't cut out this foolishness. They're definitely spying on me. Do they suspect something?

For nothing do I wait with more longing than the unimaginable happiness of a transformation. That's why at the opera I can hardly wait for things to finally get started, for the curtain to rise, because then it always feels at least a little bit like being invisible.

My mother takes me with her because my father always has an excuse for why he can't go. And my sister, as you already know, she won't go because of her retainer. I'm grateful to both of them for being so difficult.

I love operas, don't you? Since you're supposed to be disappointed in God and would rather not talk about it, we could talk about operas. No one in my family ever had even the least bit of interest in talking about operas with me, not even on vacation. How's that for lousy. There are eighty-six thousand operas, I learned it from an encyclopedia. Did you know that? Well, that's a rough estimate, but still. What I mean is, I don't think we'll run out of stuff to talk about.

I'm making progress. Soon, I figure in about two, three months, I'll have saved up enough money to be able to buy an opera guide, the best there is, with examples from scores and plot summaries and photos. I'm excited. You should see the sacrifices I'm making; my father gives me some pocket money every time I get a good grade. I'm turning into an overachiever, I can hardly believe it myself, and I used to be solidly below average in pretty much every subject. But I swear I'll let things slip again just as soon as I can manage it.

And now I'll tell you a secret. My decision is firm. I want— please don't laugh at me—I want to be an opera singer. Seriously, I'm sure of it.

By the way, did you know that Hemingway's mother was an opera singer?

But now, before I forget again, one last question, the very last question, the most crucial question of all. Do you even like children? Do you have any yourself? If you do, then it could be that you love children but don't like them, can't stand them, especially not the ones who can't stand themselves. To be honest, it's the same with me. I don't like children, I don't like myself either, not often, really almost never. So if you felt able to give an honest answer and to confide the truth in me, as far as this goes, I promise I would listen with the utmost understanding.

You see, I can't stop, and I apologize. Not even the good Lord would have the patience to listen to all of this. It really is hard, once you've gotten into it.

Our good dreamer kept writing, writing, and writing, page after page; his hand hurt. If he was really planning on sending his missive off, signed and franked, he would have wound up with a thick little parcel to carry to the post office. I assume, however, that this wasn't the point at all, or not anymore, he might in fact have completely forgotten that he'd ever intended to send it off, what with his struggle against God and the world, against family and school, against the hopelessness of finding even a single person to confide in, to say nothing of finding someone who might understand him. There was no such person, and so he had invented one. Should I, he writes, talk about operas with my sister's rabbit? Why not, actually? I'll read to him from the opera guide as soon as I have the book, I'll sing arias to him. I'll do something the world has never seen, I'll train a rabbit, who my sister named Carrot, which figures, but yes, I'll train him to be a singer. Just wait!

He hovered as he wrote the letter, as he couldn't stop writing it, like a cloud over the things in his life, like a storm cloud, so it seemed to him, even if all he had done was lock himself in the bathroom again.

He dug his heels in, planned an escape, threw the plan out, spoke only softly, scarcely audible, forbade himself to show feelings, cried no more tears.

The more he wrote, with each new page, the more despairing, the more discouraged it sounded, only sometimes interrupted by parentheses where he presented himself as a tough guy, as someone who was confident he wouldn't let things get him down. There were some passages where he even made fun of himself. He was stubborn in his efforts not to let any self-pity creep in. Should what he set down on paper be found someday, long after his death, as he imagined it, then he wanted recognition. Buried, in a patch of forest, with a certain verve, left to himself, untended, at ease.

We read that the trips he would take with his mother to the opera were called off when his father—who couldn't be made to summon any sympathy for the form, who found the singing and dying onstage, the emotional outbursts offered in return for a colossal expenditure of time by two-ton singers, the rarely comprehensible plots hard to bear (he had after all always mocked them as being "schmaltz")—took his place, for disciplinary reasons, as he explained, so that his son could come to his senses, get the gloom out of his head, have done with this withdrawal from everything that made up a normal existence, and which he, an engineer by training, found so difficult to grasp. Forced into a suit, his hair parted, a golden watch on his wrist, he looked so miserable you had to laugh. I wish him, wrote the son—and this he underlined and punctuated with exactly three exclamation points—three *appallingly* boring hours. Let him suffer, let him take years off his life just sitting there.

Then he's writing about water again, sees himself stepping up to the edge of a seaside cliff, in his head a few inchoate thoughts that he's anxious to set down on paper. The pencil is too small for the enormity of the ocean he gazes upon, but he doesn't give up, which leads to breathless, awkward lines about whatever it is a child of his age imagines infinity to be. He feels he can comprehend it, enter into it, into the mass of water spreading out below him and before him, glittering in the darkness, churned up by the last breaths of the drowned, growing darker and darker as it nears the horizon. He stands there for a long time, as the twilight deepens and the sky above grows black and blacker. What he sees twinkling out there are the running lights of the fishing boats, which he takes for floating stars.

Even farther out, he can see it, the present ends, and with it any last rational explanations.

His desire to bow before everything dark, inscrutable, monstrous, in so many words the authority of the inexplicable, is of course completely nonsensical, but soon so irresistible that he gives in to it with eyes open wide. If there is anything missing here, then it's a witness. What is shining out there could be gold, people tell stories of such things, accounts have been written—the polished gold stored in sailing ships sunk to the bottom of the ocean, foundered in storms, scuttled in sea battles, burned up under the bombardment of enemy cannons; the gold of sailors spellbound by unholy spirits, brought back to shambling, decomposing life by evil magic; gold whose reflection radiates up to the surface.

The child takes what he sees seriously, this you can tell. He's lost all interest in his little impertinences, has apparently broken off contact with his family, has forgotten what it was he wanted to be, there's nothing you wouldn't think him capable of now.

I imagine you've figured it out by now that I've taken a liking to the little guy, he's got chutzpah. The way he takes his wristwatch off and throws it over the cliff impresses me. I have no use for you anymore, you digits and hands, you hours, minutes, seconds. You can see it in his face, that's what contentment looks like. Why couldn't he have been this smart sooner? Still, kid, watch out, don't start feeling too light, lighter even than air. Don't end up believing you can fly. There's no life up there.

I can forgive him the thing about wanting to be an opera singer. It happens.

Other than that, I can't say much bad about him. He loves his mother, takes his father for a fool—children have a sixth sense for these things.

With the watch he threw off the cliff, we both think, he finally did everything right.

But now he's in a hurry to get back to safety, takes a big step back from the cliff, turns around and walks away, as if he had an appointment with another era, walks with a grace that invigorates him, walks like he won't stop walking until he's invisible.

I want to offer you, dear Suvorin, another memory, one of my student years, long ago, very long ago, in particular the memory of one of my professors, an impressive man, a philosopher. A seminar of his I took had the following name, which to this day I find unforgettable, which is why I'm able to set it down verbatim. Here it is: "The Mammoth Desire for Thought in Its Raw State."

What made me think of it? Well now, that's what a child like my little fellow, close as a brother to me, that's what he must have been feeling back then, when he stood at the edge of that cliff, just a step away from the drop.

A child, Suvorin, whom you're familiar with—of that I'm certain.

I hold here in my hand a slip of paper I've been looking for, which I found on my desk just in time, just before I finished this letter to you. It's a line from a song, an Irish one I think. Since I know how good your command of the language is, I'll give it to you in English:

Water is the strong stuff / It carries whales and ships.

XII

WHO'S SUPPOSED TO
BELIEVE THAT?

You only ever find what you weren't looking for, isn't that what they say? He's looking for a newspaper, not today's newspaper, of course, and finds an envelope, no writing on it, and opens it. Postcards, a whole stack of them. This is good. He loves postcards; all his life, no matter how old he was, he considered them a beautiful, sometimes a very beautiful thing. They were there for looking at, not for sending away.

It was one of his habits, all his life he never fell out of it: buying postcards in a new, foreign city. If anyone was going away on a trip, he would beg them, he must have been about five, to bring back postcards for him. There was no one among his relations who didn't know what joy they could bring to little Yurotschka with a picture postcard, and this set off a chain reaction. His grandparents were exempt, since they never went anywhere anymore, but not his aunts and uncles, who in turn had let their friends know.

A collection emerged, and grew.

Today he couldn't say what happened to them. He still had them when Stalin died. He was eight then. When he moved from Leningrad to Moscow, he left them with his mother, safe in good hands. When his mother died, he had other things on his mind than securing his postcard collection. Then opportunity came in the form of a few trips, first within the Soviet Union, then abroad as well, and now he had his hands full. He used every minute of his free time obtaining lots of pretty picture postcards. Back in his apartment, which was still a small one then, he spread his treasures out before him—and that's when he remembered. Just where were they, the cards he had collected as a child and young boy? The stack was lost. Thinking back on it didn't help. Not even the house he grew up in was still standing.

But now there he is, Beethoven. The stone Beethoven from Karlovy Vary. One, two, three, twelve postcards. Always the same, faintly colored motif. Beethoven storms off into the storm. On closer examination, you have to admit that Beethoven is not only bearing up against the storm, he's got the upper hand. And it's funny, too. In the summer, when not the faintest breeze is stirring, even then Beethoven storms off into the storm. You get a sense of the eternal. The stone, you think, from which his body was carved, might crumble, but Beethoven would survive this, too.

Suvorin, quite the child again, spreads all twelve postcards out on the table in front of him in his kitchen. Beforehand, he wiped clean the oilcloth spread over the table. Nothing worse than grease stains on a postcard. He has washed his hands as well.

He must, he thinks, have had something in mind to have bought so many at once, but he's forgotten what it was. Now all he wants—what else did he have to do that day—is to take advantage of this bounty. He looks for something suitable to write with, finds only the unsuitable: dried-up felt-tip pens, ballpoint pens with no ink, pencils with broken lead, two no-longer-functional fountain pens. He spends a long time looking without finding what he's after, until, in the kitchen, in the utensil drawer, a small pen catches his eye, pink ink, which he immediately tries out.

Now he can get to work. He would put an address on every single postcard—and then come up with something to write. There are people who think that behind every trivial thing there's some allusion that they don't understand. Just like there are people who never stop bothering you, even when they're not saying anything.

But as soon as he gets comfortable in his chair at the kitchen table, he begins to have second thoughts. To whom should they be sent? Does he have their names right? Do they still live at the addresses that he must still have written down somewhere in one of his address books? He couldn't be sure of that, but to look them all up would take quite a while. Does he even know enough people whom he can stand and to whom he would also enjoy writing? And the addressees, how will they react? Would the arrival of a postcard sent by him not cause confusion for this or that person, especially since he had never before honored anyone with correspondence of this kind? Wouldn't they have to assume he was pursuing some specific purpose, preparing the way for a request, that he wanted to ask them for money, was planning something, like a surprise comeback as a pianist performing Beethoven's sonatas? They would get curious, want to know more and, oh Lord, call—except of course for those for whom it had long been a cherished custom to doubt his sanity.

All of this makes Suvorin tired. He retreats, for the time being, into the secure realm of his bedroom.

In a park in Karlovy Vary, on twelve postcards, and now also inside his head, Beethoven storms off into the storm. It's not just an image, it's a state of being, life-sized and set in stone.

Outside of Vienna, at the presbytery in Nussdorf, there's another statue that's almost identical, though it's difficult to know for sure without direct comparison. I assume that there are even more of them scattered around in other places, impressive as they are. For once, a statue of someone who's not high up on horseback. No winner of battles, this; though, really, triumph was Beethoven's true career. What it is, there at the presbytery and over in Karlovy Vary, is a monument to self-assertion! One against all! Next door at the Pfarrwirt restaurant sit the Viennese, drinking wine and eating pork fat, and well they might. Sometimes there's someone plucking a zither.

Suvorin, before he turns the lights off behind him, reserves a Beethoven for himself, so to speak: he pins one of the postcards to the door of his icebox with a magnet. Eleven Beethovens remain at his disposal.

Weariness, he can feel it, has gathered within him, greater than the weight of man. He will decide which people he can send a postcard to after he's slept and is able to think about it. For now, he's far too worked up. Where did this idea come from, what was he thinking? And besides that, what was he ever going to come up with that could fit on such tiny cards, made for nothing more than a brief greeting? Never once had he taken a postcard, put an address, a message, and a stamp on it, and tossed it in a mailbox; they were, for him, collectors' items, meant to be hoarded. He took joy in this. Other people collected other things—coins, insects, butterflies. So his family wasn't greatly concerned. He was met with goodwill, they told themselves the boy probably wants to be a painter someday, maybe an architect, an explorer.

The temperature has fallen overnight, and a cold, biting wind has swept in. This is no rarity in the autumn. To expect windows to close tight would be too much to ask, even in Vienna.

He kept his coat on in bed, and his wool socks, too, and not for the first time.

The next morning the postcards lie waiting for him, like cards in a game of solitaire.

His breakfast consists of two spoonfuls of honey, and after that, still refreshed from his morning swim, he prepares some vegetables for lunch, which, when it's time to eat, he will steam. Dinner requires no great effort to prepare, he contents himself with chocolate, one or two bars.

Beethoven wasn't a walker, although he was capable and robust enough to cover great distances on foot. He took a carriage from Vienna to Baden, but between villages he walked, literally marched, blowing off steam. For some of those who encountered him of an evening in the streets of Gumpoldskirchen, or Tattendorf, it was an uncanny sight. Beethoven, picked up as a "suspicious character"—there are stories. Two provincial policemen arrest a man, bring him in to the watchhouse. Someone who wouldn't think of carrying identification. He is Beethoven, he informs them. Who's supposed to believe that? They take Beethoven for a nutcase posing as Beethoven. He's been drinking, which he makes no attempt to deny. The room is cramped. In the small watchhouse there's only one other room, even smaller, best known among the cheerful tipplers in town as the drunk tank. They lock the raging man in. They can't see any signs of him calming down, keep an eye out for reinforcements, which then arrive, more by chance than anything, in the form of a farmer; his wife, he says, has locked him out.

If the man really is the famed composer, there's only one person in these parts who could confirm or deny his claim. They send the farmer off with the promise that they'll deal with him as soon as possible once the task at hand is completed. And anyway his wife will probably have calmed down in the meantime.

The organist from the nearby Stift Heiligenkreuz monastery, pulled out of bed well past midnight, confirms Beethoven's identity, gives the all-clear.

Suvorin picks up the pink pen and one of the postcards and writes with a smile and a steady hand the following sentences:

Beethoven, see reverse, on his way into history. He's off to murder Ivan the Terrible, murderer of music.

Please, I ask him, send me that one. Postpaid by recipient.

He tackles a second postcard, one to his daughter, a political scientist working as an official in Brussels. If it can be avoided, it says, don't marry an American.

His daughter is unable to see a connection between Beethoven and her father's request.

XIII

Since Suvorin, like so many Russians, is superstitious, chapter thirteen has to a large extent been dispensed with. Time for a moment of contemplation, a snapshot of the pianist on his own. Suvorin sits—quite surprisingly for all those who think they know him—at a computer. I'm baffled, too. Looks like a thirteen, like bad luck. He's a man of sound. If he doesn't hear anything, he doesn't see anything. Even when he still gave concerts, he was a listener among the other listeners, among all those who listened to him—the most important one. He could never get anything past his ears. They didn't waste a lot of time on pleasantries. No matter how enthusiastically his appearances were hailed in the papers the next day, his ears were the more honest witnesses; they told him if on this or that evening, in Milan or Budapest, he wasn't good enough.

You can't silence your inner voices just by stopping up your ears. There were times when it was bad, and times when it was worse. Sometimes it seemed to him as though his entire body, every pore on his skin were an ear. But that's when it could happen. He couldn't count on it, it wasn't a sure thing, but from time to time it happened, on this or that evening he would succeed in surpassing his own capabilities, and when it happened it turned the evening into a cause for celebration.

Although I have two ears, he liked to say, they are always of one mind.

Then, when he stopped leaving the house, when he barely

bothered opening a window, there was his "music box." The dial has been turned to the same spot for years, or, better yet: has rested there, on 92.0 FM, the classical station. It's on non-stop, or nearly; at most, he'll turn the volume down a little. And now this.

He wishes his faithful friend good luck, and turns it off.

Although there's no semblance of pleasant reverie, and nothing about him that seems relaxed, Suvorin seems to be having fun with his digital explorations. What interests him about this activity is what he calls the "astronautical," a thing unheard of for a man of his ilk. He feels like he's flying to the moon, or has already landed on it. Unreal terrain. Advanced technology. A virtual cosmos. He's so excited that his hands are cold.

What a sight! A beginner struggles with an all-rounder. We'll see, he says after a good month or so, and tries to buck himself up. At some point, dear sir, it will be I who has you by the tail.

The computer was a gift from his daughter, who hoped it would be a way that she and her father could keep in touch. She could write him emails, he could write back. The long-interrupted conversation between them—a conversation that had never actually begun—could, albeit in makeshift fashion, be resumed.

But Suvorin had little interest in this. He wrote no emails, which is to say he didn't reply to his daughter's, which turned the whole well-intentioned gesture into a travesty and just caused more worry on her part. What was wrong with him, why didn't he answer? Could a second stroke be ruled out? Before she had moved abroad because of her career, she had offered to buy him a cell phone—which he had flatly refused.

She put the effort in. She was the daughter she'd always wanted to be. This way we can talk. And we have to talk.

We only have to do what we want to do, groused her father. And I don't want to.

Just like mine, my dad, he doesn't want to either, a friend said to her. Give him a computer, but don't ask him beforehand. That's what I did.

And now Suvorin the musician sits at a table late into the night, intimidated but impressed, his eyes close to the screen, feeling his way forward in a labyrinth of numbers and letters; like playing the piano, all you need are your fingers, actually just your index finger. What new language has been concocted here, what libraries erected and torn down? Glowing images leap out at him, and invitations to view further images, books, atlases—archives of visual phenomena.

It was impressive, this jungle with its ever-growing vege-tation. But something is missing! And it doesn't take long till Suvorin knows what it is. The perfect moment! The one perfect moment! The rare, the unrepeatable, the most precious thing for any musician. If that wasn't a reason to fold your hands!

Doesn't exist on the internet, not on a screen.

How much there is to know, he comforts himself, although he has always doubted the power of knowledge, and more still the power of the knowledgeable.

A man lost in the vastness of the web. A man who talks to a machine like a child talks to the water into which he has cast his line.

XIV

A DIFFERENT KIND OF PAST?

When the telephone rang and I picked up the receiver and heard a voice start speaking on the other end, which, because it was very quiet and hard to understand, I recognized as Suvorin's, it certainly came as a surprise. He'd never called me before. Neither could I remember having given him my phone number. But this was followed by yet another surprise, a much bigger one. He would like, he said, to introduce me to his new girlfriend.

Come again?

She's very petite, he said. What's the word? Handy? Yes, handy. Very handy, even, and very elegant. But it's not easy to figure her out, to understand how she works.

How women work? Surely he doesn't think that I can be of any help to him there? But of course I agreed to a meeting. When?

The usual place?

Fine, fine, when?

Sunday, two o'clock?

This was a good week away, time I could use to get myself accustomed to the thought that I would be meeting a man newly in love, almost a miracle in itself, but all the more so when the man was of an age better suited to safer occupations than subjecting oneself to the incalculable risks of a newly kindled love affair. Had he not repeatedly complained that his doctors had advised him against any form of excitement? How does a sick man deal with love? The body can't be expected to perceive arousal as an immediate danger to its health; does he therefore, having fallen in love, feel only bliss? In such an emotional state, the head, as we know, is relieved of its command, it ceases to function. But then again, maybe it's precisely this unhealthy excitement that makes him realize he's fallen in love? How transformed will the Suvorin who presents himself to me on Sunday be? Will a fashionable scarf adorn his neck? Will a hat (instead of the cap he usually wears) convey the news that, even for him, it's not all over?

To bid welcome to a late, last youth—this form of homesickness had never occurred to him. He would neither have considered it possible nor, in all likelihood, have thought it desirable. The bright, clear winter light that envelops the lover at the end of his life. And yet it's not without warmth. Better not to even begin to expose yourself to the authority of the know-it-alls. If what has apparently happened here is laughable, why not laugh with it? Don't they get to laugh in heaven, on every rung of the ladder that leads up there?

To be honest, I have a strong aversion to late passions. The second spring, as they call such a condition, doesn't turn old men young. They end up, most of them, as even more pitiable creatures than they were before. But still, I thought, once the news has made the rounds, at least he won't have to put up with any applause.

I don't want to act as though I thought of nothing else all week. I saw a production of *La Bohème* where the producers had hit upon the idea of making the artists a gang of pot-smoking failures; Rodolfo coughed and Mimi read the newspaper. At the sight of the leaves beginning to turn, I gave myself over to thoughts that would cause any but a strong soul to despair. I wrote letters to Palermo, Dresden, Ansbach. Finally, pomegranates at the market again, I immediately stocked up. I ate meat again, for the first time in a long while, a delicious, tender cut of beef imported from Latin America. The girl who helped me out of my coat and hung it up in the cloakroom had a book lying open in front of her whose title was *Die Liebe ist ein schlechter Verlierer*—"Love is a bad loser." And as I sat reading, which I like to do on evenings I spend alone, my thoughts again turned back to Suvorin. How could they not, after a line like the following:

"If a man does not keep pace with his companions, perhaps it is because he hears a different drummer. Let him step to the music which he hears, however measured or far away."

You could talk books with Suvorin. He knew his Russians, anyway. He loved the writers of his homeland more than the composers.

He loved deep pockets for their usefulness in allowing him to carry a slim volume of stories or poems at his side, always within reach.

And now he loved someone petite, handy, complicated? I don't know why, but on hearing that description I couldn't help but think of the young Asian women Vienna is positively teeming with these days. Those who don't disappear into the city's red-light districts are studying music. Is it beyond imagining that an old, lonely man, who was anything but an ordinary old, lonely man, could have fallen in love with one of his students? Or she with him? Why not, all things considered. Her falling in love with him I consider more likely. It's not hard to think up reasons. A highly gifted talent, when it comes to technique she's got it all, good nerves, pretty to look at—still a child, really, it shows in her eyes, which is precisely what makes the thing complicated. Yes, such a story could plausibly be told along those lines. Her playing lacks maturity, to say nothing of depth, she heard someone say once. Afterward not a day or night goes by without her being reminded of this. It torments her. I have no depth. She hears it herself now. Depth is what's lacking. Depth has its own tones, a music that she can't yet hear. She can't hear the stillness, the disturbing, uncanny stillness of the depths. Ready to sacrifice everything, including a sensible diet, she soon stops speaking entirely, until the silence she produces frightens her. Her parents, too, who have come from far away, are frightened by their daughter. They're especially bewildered by the black sheets on her bed, black like the finish on a grand piano. The explanation that the color has something to do with the depth of her nightly repose they don't understand, they remain mistrustful. But her mother can be pacified with a piece by Mozart, her father by a hug.

Never has she worked longer and harder in her search for depth. Who, if not a Russian, would know something about it? What, if not love, could help her to break through? Best of all would be an impossible love, a reckless love that places her soul at the mercy of unknown dangers, overwhelms her, tears her apart. She needs, it becomes clear to her, a catastrophe. She is serious about this, she needs a teacher, the right teacher, and a real drama. How can you conquer the depths if you don't have the courage to let yourself fall?

Thus does a little affair such as this come to be, an affair that begins to sound interesting precisely because it offers nothing lewd, nothing sordid. Is it then good enough, pure enough, interesting enough for someone like Suvorin? Oh, I don't know. I still don't really think him capable of an affair of this caliber. Maybe he just has it all mixed up, has mistaken a woman for a book, love for a poem, a hat on his head for happiness? With him, the best approach, and this I've suspected from the first time we met, is to be prepared for anything.

I arrive punctually at La Gondola and have a seat, as agreed, looking out through the large windows, spotting him after a few minutes, observing how difficult it can be to cross from one side of the street to the other. Only then does it occur to me that he's alone. No doubt about it, he's come alone.

It must show on my face. What's wrong? You look like there's something the matter?

Oh no, no, everything's fine, totally fine. More than fine, even, better than if my fears were justified and he'd arrived with a pretty young thing who sat there adoring him with her almond eyes, her conquest, her savior. My story—assuming the diver in the depths wasn't going to surface after all—is mere nonsense, a figment of my imagination. I am, however, by no means ashamed. I could serve you up other versions in an instant, stories you wouldn't believe, stories that are of comparable fanatic clarity, but I'll skip it, I think. For now, I'm just happy to see the old man sitting at the table with me.

You look good, I say, good and refreshed.

You're lying, but that makes no difference. Thank you anyway. Lies come hard on the heels of truth. A proverb. Do you know it?

Lies have short legs, I answer, that's how I learned it.

Crooked legs, he does me one better, and crooked noses. I had a teacher like that, a highly regarded educator, someone I particularly admired. And then he was gone, you understand? They came for him. He didn't want to accept the truth. Music will protect me, he said. It didn't. People always forget this. That the sun still rises over the earth.

His eyes search the table—for what? The menu? If so, it would be the first time he'd picked one up. Is he considering whether the thing that just surfaced from his memory could be chased off by a cigarette?

I had only ever seen him like this when he spoke of his wife—sad, pensive.

I'm searching, he explains, and underscores this statement with a nod. He's searching for what? It is, I can feel it, a special moment that I'm witnessing. Is he searching for the right face? A particular grave in a cemetery? A different kind of past?

I leave him be.

He searches for whatever it may be for a while longer, keeps nodding his head, places his hands on the menu in front of him. Then he looks up. Music is made by people, but people are, for music, a matter of indifference. I was too young to contradict him. It wouldn't have been right, not even if someone's life were at stake.

Never was I so happy to see a waiter.

Is there something I can bring the gentleman? he asked.

Suvorin ordered tap water.

A cappuccino for the gentleman as well, I say. And I'll take one, too, and another tap water! Thank you.

Suvorin is taken aback, he looks at me and smiles. How did you know I wanted a cappuccino? You can read minds?

I deny it. If offered the ability, I would refuse. Just another thing to put up with! Even more information. Even more control. What's going on in that head of yours, my darling? I'd have to be an idiot to want to know. Which brings us right back to lying.

Dangerous people, Suvorin says, people who were paid well for their crimes. He's sure not making it easy for me today, I think. What crimes?

Reading other people's minds.

Wouldn't it be more entertaining if we had another person at the table with us, the aforementioned young Asian woman, for example, just bursting with happiness? Didn't he tell me she was coming?

A week ago you called me and promised me a surprise, do you remember?

I remember.

A new girlfriend.

I remember. He nods. I remember quite well. And?

His hand disappears into his deep pockets and produces something that looks like a camera. And is one! Brand-new, he says with noticeable pride, and adds, after a deep breath: *brand spanking new*—a difficult phrase, not one he's used to, he seems visibly delighted to have pronounced it correctly.

Here there's something I should note: his mania for encyclopedias and dictionaries! And not for the ones meant for a lady's handbag, but the big, heavy tomes, handsomely bound if you can get them, like the ones you can still find in used bookshops, albeit less and less often. Together with his few Italian textbooks they took up whole meters of shelf space, there to prepare for occasions that would hopefully arrive someday, especially the books in German. He read them like other people read thrillers. He stopped only when he was too drunk or he was pressed for time and, still not exactly sober, had to turn his attention to a score waiting for him to crack it open. The study of the German language in general and of specific words in particular drove away other, unwelcome thoughts. He underlined them with a marker, the tricky ones, the ones that were difficult for him at first, that could be pronounced only with effort, patience, and practice. Words like *Funkelnagelneu*. Like *Haarnadelkurve*. Like *Blaubeerkuchen*, "blueberry pastry"—the baking of which isn't an art, per se, but then again, ultimately, is. His wife had a knack for it; how he liked to be around her whenever she was working with flour and eggs! It drove him wild, how powerfully she moved her arms, how she dug her hands into the dough; he was smitten. She was so much in her element baking that sometimes she hummed softly to herself and moved her hips like she was dancing. She got embarrassed if she felt she was being

watched, and scolded him. Go see to your Bartók or your books!
He couldn't get anywhere with her, not in the kitchen, where
she was waiting for the oven, not her husband, to heat up. And as
for blueberry pastry, for her it was still called what it had always
been called, *chernichny pirog*, nothing else.

He had fun with new words and the things he could think
up to go with them: *knallhart* and *knallvoll*, which he imagined
as two quarrelsome siblings; the hefty pop of a little word like
fuchsteufelswild or a strange silvery gem like *mucksmäuschenstill*,
"quiet as a mouse," which Suvorin, he couldn't help it, wanted
to pronounce that way as well, quiet as a mouse, softly, almost
tenderly, as if he didn't want to scare any of the little critters off.
His Sunday words! He wrote them down in one of his spiral
notebooks. He put whole lists together to get his tongue and
lips used to them when he read them aloud. He practiced them
through repetition, as he had once done in his childhood at the
piano with a finger exercise or fugue.

And so he kept at it. The German language—tough dough!

The way his hands are shaking I'm afraid his new purchase
might slip from his grasp and fall to the floor. In his hands, I
have seen, no cup is safe, no glass either, nor the spectacles that
he puts on, takes off, puts on; that he adjusts before taking them
off again. And now this camera, which he regards with obvious
pleasure. My new Japanese girlfriend! he says.

Well, all right, I wasn't completely off the mark. Nor, by the
way, was what he told me. The thing is in fact petite, handy,
and, understandably enough, complicated. A camera, an expensive item, a digital camera from Canon, the latest model.

Even if instead of a new lover he's now showing me a camera,
my central question is still justified: What in God's name is a
man like him thinking, at his age? Why make such a purchase—

it can't have been cheap! Is it Suvorin who is searching for depth, after all?

What are you going to do with it? I ask.

You're the one who's going to be doing something with it. I'll show you how to work the thing.

And this he does, in great detail. He must have studied every page of the user's manual with a magnifying glass, must have learned the whole thing by heart, even taken some photos himself already. A toy whose technology I'd have thought someone like him least capable of mastering. I'm amazed, but still I ask myself if he might have done better investing the money in a new set of teeth? Or spending it on a week in San Remo?

I don't want to spoil his fun, so I don't mention that I'm completely useless when it comes to cameras, cell phones, and all the rest of it. A child can figure them out, but not me, which for my part I count as a big plus. I refuse to participate. I don't even like to talk on the phone. I'm a carrier-pigeon man, a man of in-person conversations during which you look the other person in the eye—a man who relies on his memory, unassisted.

A glass that Suvorin tries to push to one side to make room as he hands his camera to me tips over and falls to the floor.

A waiter rushes over. Please, sir, let me get it, no problem.

I apologize by ordering more coffee.

Meanwhile a young man has appeared in the doorway, a somewhat undernourished, almost gaunt, but good-looking kid who scans the whole room and then makes his way toward our table. He is noticeably pale, sickly. (Do as the Russians do, Suvorin will advise him in conversation later on, eat everything that's unhealthy, and lots of it, cake, chocolate—so long as there's sugar!) Most noticeable of all is his hair, a real gift of a mane: a tangle of tight curls, firm as braids, which no comb could tame, no hairdresser either, a very original, magnificent head of hair, flying out in all directions, following the dictates of no fashion. And not trying to make a statement either, from the look of it. This hair declares no allegiance. This isn't some stranded hippie standing here. The rationale is probably a simple one: that here is someone who, out of love for his hair, has given up the struggle against it.

Suvorin is too caught up in the pleasure of explaining to me the functions and functionality of his new acquisition to see the young man, who politely waits to be noticed.

I help out, just as politely. One moment, I say, we'll be right with you.

This little window is what you look through. And here's the button. That's what you push. Puts everything you take a picture of into focus automatically.

And what am I supposed to take a picture of?

Well, first, the painting on the wall. Flowers and light. And then, what's about to happen. Somebody's about to come here who asked a favor of me, an actor. If I understood things right on the telephone, he's rehearsing something Russian at the Burgtheater. I assume it's something by Chekhov they're trying to put on. Yeah, well, let them. Our doctor. And he was one, too. A doctor and a poet. Doesn't happen so often these days.

And the actor is standing there, listening; is friendly, but still doesn't join in yet.

And what does he want? I ask.

To hear a Russian speaking Russian!

Suvorin doesn't seem to find it particularly amusing, or think it will make for an especial boon to the dramatic arts, or whatever the idea is. Do you ever go to the theater, he wants to know.

I shake my head.

What is it, theater—I ask you. No, I won't ask you, because I can tell you. Theater is when Austrians play Russians. That's theater!

I've never figured it out. You simply can't tell whether his laugh takes the short route through his mouth or detours through his nose. He almost chokes on it.

The only thing worse, he says, is when it's a German who's playing a Russian.

This I don't even want to imagine, not with my long-standing aversion to the theater, which I profess without any polite restraint even around theater aficionados. I suffer from an acute allergy when it comes to the theater, and haven't ever felt the desire to do anything about it. The whole theater surrounding the theater, especially here in Vienna; the papers are full of it, the theaters are full—forget it! It's annoying! Like the lady I once rented a room from was annoying with her passion for certain Viennese stage actors, these darlings of entire segments of the population—it became so intolerable that I had to get out of there. I normally react quite calmly when someone accuses me of lacking education, I even take it as a compliment. That's how I am, maybe a little full of myself, maybe even arrogant, if you like. I've never been known for being diplomatic. No, sorry, I've never read a single page of Hamsun, no, nor Dostoyevsky, and why should I subject myself to the plays of Strindberg? The unhappiness of a marriage, act one, intermission, a glass of bubbly, say hello to some friends, greet them with exaggerated effusiveness, hug, chat, and when they flicker the lights do everything all at once, make plans for later, say goodbye, finish your drink, quick stop at the can, back to your seat, the unhappiness of a marriage, act two, conclusion. Applause, of course (do you hear it, Suvorin?), oh man, they're outdoing themselves. Ovations. Curtain calls.

A successful evening!

Sure, a successful evening. No thanks.

Oh right, you haven't asked me about Proust yet, whether I—

I can't help myself. Care for a quote? From whom? From Proust, of course, let's not change the subject: "Real books should be the offspring not of daylight and casual talk but of darkness and silence."

One bit of consolation: When everyone is sitting in the theater, at least the streets are empty.

I'd be lying if I said I didn't enjoy it: I suspect I'm considered a hopeless case; and, to be honest, in these circles I'm sometimes downright determined to be just that. A gift I give myself, to have touched a nerve, as if I had maligned Western civilization. At any rate I can't complain. Somebody has to be the dumb one. My last attempt to get through an evening at the theater was fifty or more years ago, a student production that I attended only because I was in the cast.

It's music that allows me to draw closer to myself.

The young man who's about to come join us is playing a Russian here at the Burgtheater. I'm supposed to shoot him.

A nice triangle, I think. The actor in the role of an invisible man, hearing his death sentence. He's here, yet is still being waited for. I know he's there but say nothing. I calmly keep the conversation going. And why did he arrange to meet with you?

So I can help him!

Help him? With what?

We'll ask him.

He didn't say?

He was in a bind, Suvorin says. He was looking for his soul, which, you know, in the legitimate theater, you have to put your soul on the line with every emotion you try to convey. Or maybe it was more complicated than that. He was looking for the play in the language, before the director ruined it with his ideas. He was looking for the second skin that's meant to guard against routine, looking for a tone, a rhythm, a spiritual connection to the person he was playing. You know how actors talk. I don't understand a word of it. But being in a bind, that much I understand. It's five minutes before the concert is supposed to begin, I'm standing in the dressing room with my dress shirt on, and I realize that I left my cuff links at the hotel.

The actor continues to remain patiently and respectfully silent. Does he think the man he's listening to is himself an actor? Is he even wrong in thinking so? Suvorin is, after all, a master of the dramatic pause.

It's not such a stupid idea, Suvorin reflects. To feel your way into a role through the sound of a language. Can it hurt? Why should I be less friendly to someone asking me a favor than a waiter is to me?

But of course they won't be doing the play at the Burgtheater in the original, but rather in German translation. Maybe it makes no difference? The main thing is that they stay on its trail, keep searching for the Russian soul. I can't help not taking the theater seriously. Doesn't all this sound familiar to you?

Familiar, yes, and funny too. So it does exist, then—the Russian soul?

You're asking me of all people? A Russian?

He looks up, casting about for the waiter to ask for another glass of tap water, and finally notices our silent visitor.

I didn't even see you there.

Thank you for taking the time.

Here, says Suvorin, and points to the only empty chair at our table. At a table with two Germans, he jokes, well all right!

He hands me the camera, you take the photo. Me, just me. You know how my girlfriend works by now. And don't forget, after this, the painting, too. And you, he asks the actor, what is it you want me to say?

Whatever you want.

What I want? First I want a cigarette! I do have to concentrate, after all.

I find my pack and hold it out to him.

Suvorin makes use of the time it takes for him to pull out a cigarette; for him to feel he's got it sitting right between his fingers; for my Zippo to catch, which it doesn't do, because it's out of lighter fluid again; for us to get the attention of the waiter, who is serving a pizza over on the other side of the restaurant; for him to be apprised of the situation and to come back with matches, strike one and hold it out for the gentleman, who in leaning over almost knocks another glass to the floor—he makes use of these few minutes, I'm sure of it, to get used to the actor's presence. What are you doing, aside from the fact you're playing a Russian? What's the play called?

The play is called *Sunset*, by Isaac Babel.

Ah, I see, *Sunset*. A play in eight scenes. I know it. Not a bad piece. Not a bad author, this Babel, God knows. They liquidated him anyway. Killed him, just like that. Suvorin goes quiet. And then asks: What role are you playing?

A shopkeeper, Fomin.

Fomin, look here. And Suvorin begins to declaim in Russian: *We'll sing, we'll celebrate, and when it's time to die, we'll die!* Ah yes.

Anything else? asks the waiter coming over to our table.

The coffee, unfortunately, has gone cold, which isn't a complaint, Suvorin is quick to explain, though he declines to have another brought to him. He does want something else, however, and points to a glass case. There, that cake.

A *Gugelhupf*, sir?

A piece, please.

One piece of *Gugelhupf*, very good. Would the gentleman like a spot of whipped cream?

Suvorin misses the question and turns to me. Have you also noticed this? Waiters in Vienna, the things they say all day long, they can sing them better than they can say them. Also, the way they repeat everything you say?

I'm by no means a stranger to these phenomena. Nor to what happens once the waiter has brought the *Gugelhupf*. Suvorin regards the cake quite closely for some time, finds nothing to take fault with, and so begins to break it up into little pieces, which he then, piece by piece, as if he were feeding a sick bird, lets drop into his cup and then stirs, adding sugar. The porridge is ready—and so is the child who spoons it up.

One of my uncles, he says, who had no teeth left, he used to do it this way. And so got himself a new name: Uncle Porridge! Or simply: Porridge. What's with Porridge, why's he making that face? Is Porridge still asleep? What's Porridge gotten into now? Nothing, really, except for the fact that after he died they found something that turned all my aunt's hair, that is, his wife's hair, white, literally overnight. And she had been proud of not having a single gray hair at her age. The few that wouldn't cooperate she plucked out. And yet, after reading a diary her husband kept, just a few pages long, she turned into a white-haired old woman.

Suvorin is struck—as am I—by the young man's politeness, which, I notice, bothers the old pianist. If you want to play a Russian, he says, first lesson—cut that out. Russians aren't polite.

I'll take that into consideration.

To picture Suvorin when he's like this, it helps to imagine a man in front of a hut, legs outstretched, resting on a little bench, smoking and daydreaming a little, while he watches a wall of heavy black clouds that the wind is blowing past the horizon. Far away, in the next village, a storm is brewing. Far away, a dog barks. The Moscow the three sisters dream of is closer.

XV

A SINGLE BEAUTIFUL FIGURE?

Suvorin seemed pensive today, but there were so many potential reasons for this that I didn't even want to guess. It couldn't have been the weather, anyway, since the sky was blue, the air dry, the temperature comfortable. It had snowed, and—oh, miracle for Vienna—the snow had stuck; there it lay just as lightly as it had fallen, on the streets and on the sidewalks, you felt like you could just blow it away. It coated the branches of the trees. Even the sun seemed pleased.

A woman carried a birdcage out of a shop.

A child squirmed free from its stroller so that it could stare at another child in a sled pulled by a young father—and then considered, or so it seemed, whether it should save its screaming for later or go ahead and let loose.

Our two waiters looked out the window with arms crossed over their chest, they, too, lost in thought. It wasn't lunchtime customers they were looking for, at any rate.

Suvorin stared straight ahead.

They were mysterious, untamed, confused thoughts, he couldn't get them out of his head, and in all likelihood—that's how it'll end up being, he thought—they were completely worthless.

That morning, he said after a while, sounding very bewildered, he had woken up on the floor next to his bed.

This experience seemed abominable to him.

I could say, well, sure, it had to happen sometime. I'm probably not the only one to ever fall out of his bed, that much I'm sure of. And in the end it's hardly a tragedy, but still, it's unusual, especially in my case. I went to bed, this I remember, and fell asleep, but then, and this is a fact, I woke up next to the bed, and that without my noticing anything, without my sleep being disturbed in the least. I wasn't even cold. Yet the location of my body would have led you to expect otherwise.

Not even when I was young did this sort of thing happen to me, he said after a while. If I came to on the floor after a night of drinking at a bar or in a friend's apartment, I was certain of having fallen asleep in precisely that spot. If I made it back home and into my own bed, then I woke up in my bed.

Suvorin was at a loss. What kind of person falls out of bed—sober, and on top of that without waking up? I obviously didn't hurt myself either. No injuries, no bumps, not even a scratch.

He moved his hands, his arm, his shoulders, swiveled his head around. Today of all days not even my back hurts. It's nice, if also bizarre! On the other hand, just what kind of creature am I? A healthy person would at least have a headache after such a night.

Not only did I not wake up during my brief journey from bed to floor, I also apparently kept on dreaming, without the slightest interruption—the last thing I need, uninterrupted dreams! I was playing piano, see, and not even that badly. Still, it smelled like chicken soup. You never feel full. You feel hot, but you don't feel full. You throw open the window, get hypothermia, and fall into bed—if you weren't already lying in it. How absurd it all is. After I fell to the floor I just kept playing, albeit unwillingly, since I've forbidden myself from dreaming anything that has to do with music. But what can you do.

I didn't interrupt. I accepted that I was witness to a conversation he was having with himself, half in Russian, half in

German, and again I thought that I should, as I have so often planned to do, take it upon myself to learn Russian someday. I could ask Anna, Olga, Nora. Why not ask Suvorin? The only thing that's gotten in the way is my indolence. To this day, I haven't even managed to get hold of a dictionary. I can't figure myself out.

Now just one of the two waiters remained at the window, looking out, watching with a quiet, childlike joy the snow falling again in heavy flakes. Each snowflake a white angel, he'll tell his little daughter when he gets home from work. I've seen her.

I would rather have played pool than the piano. Or a game of chess. I'd have sent the knight jumping all over the board. The knight was always my favorite piece. How I liked to play the rider!

He thought for a moment. I could go look in on Schiff again, the cellist, he doesn't live far from here, everybody takes him for an unfriendly person, no idea why. He's not, not at all. People just like to talk. Like they talk about everybody else, probably, me included. Like they talk about musicians whom nobody can force to only ever talk about music. Let them. We just happen to like it, not trying to be liked by everyone. Or as he puts it: Keep on being a normal person and you'll have trouble!

He has a spacious apartment spread out over two floors with a staircase connecting them, and so has room enough for a pool table, a Brunswick imported from the United States, and it doesn't just sit there either, an impressive, pretty piece of décor. It's there to be played on. "Knocking some balls around," as he calls the game—a child, borne in the wombs of mathematics, music, and poetry. He can't fantasize or philosophize enough over this showpiece of a pool table, or what do I know what he does, thinks up stories, plays around with ideas based on these stories. He gets to be very funny while he's doing it, very passionate—really silly, I should say. Like how the last time I visited he asked me (and asked himself) who it was who actually fathered this three-hundred-kilo monster. A nobleman? His carpenter? An Italian cloth merchant? What man wouldn't want to get in on it, to be the lover chosen by luck, by secret dreams, offered up to the desires of three women at once, who have appeared before him as a single beautiful figure?

Those who want to see Schiff in a good mood, however, shouldn't take things too seriously or try to turn the game into a competition; shouldn't try to shine, boast, be ambitious; in short: should give themselves over to a ritual, not play to win.

We've spoken about it every now and then, said Suvorin, when I was over for a visit, just what it was that was so interesting about the desire to win, no matter in what context and by what means. Long conversations without any real conclusion. Unless it was this: At some point, at least when you're under your own roof, you have to put an end to everything that is so agonizing about our profession: rivalry, competition, struggle. Who had a good day, who had a bad one. They don't put a pool table up onstage. But try to get that out of your head.

The worst ones, says Schiff, are the conqueror types, who turn each game into a tournament, each concert into a struggle—the killjoys at the conductor's stand who wave the queue around like a baton. How little feeling, how little sensitivity they have. They do what they always do. They play to play themselves up. And they talk the whole time! Conductors who talk! They know everything, but they don't know a thing. I can't hear you, one of them said to me once. You're conducting too loud, I told him. A strong guy like you, I heard him say to the first violin, talking past me. What did I do? I played even quieter, took all my strength and played even quieter. I mean I knew what my instrument was capable of, the sounds it could make, even with just the slightest touch of the bow. And all of this after an endless flight across the Atlantic, after imprisonment in a hotel room with windows that you can't open, which with me always leads first to a fit of rage and then, sure enough, to a cold. If you're not lucky, and of course you're not, it couldn't be any other way, you have to deal with a conductor, young, jovial, a little cocky for my taste, self-importance incarnate, a star conductor, as they had assured me when the contracts were being signed and the name wasn't confirmed yet, which of course doesn't mean a thing, since in the States everybody's a star, soon as they start acting like it, the newspapers write it, the audience believes it, and we're the ones on the hook for it!

Callas would have bitten his head off, one of the musicians in the orchestra assured me after rehearsal, an older, elegant, distinguished gentleman, a dyed-in-the-wool Italian.

I was quiet for a moment, picturing her to myself, jaws opened like a tigress, ready to pounce—there are photos of her to match. Oh yes, that she would have!

I was truly moved by the solace that my colleague clearly wanted to give me, and I let him know how grateful I was. I think I even hugged him. I think I even heard his heartbeat. Really it was only for his sake that I played an encore, which otherwise I never do.

Some conductors, when you work with them, it's like lying on air; with others you're lying on rocks. There are those who walk and those who glide. Such is fate.

Yes, I said. It did me good, listening to Richter. I knew it would help me.

I sat there at ease, happy. Not entirely happy, if I'm honest. Now we'd gone and done it, instead of knocking a few balls around, we'd started talking about what the work makes of us, about what we might be capable of making of our work.

They must have sent this guy over from Hollywood, the way he presented himself, and of course maybe he was the right man for the soaring music they have in movies, could be—always on a collision course with kitsch, they give me a stomachache. Big gestures, big bluster! By that point I didn't care one way or another if I could be heard or not. I couldn't help thinking of what my teacher had told me. The quieter you play, the better they can hear you.

Right, right, I thought, well said! But how do you do it when your vision is going black from the sheer mass of thick, heavy notes? Triple forte! Dear merciful Lord! But it was all behind me now, of course, which my friend, in his excitement, had apparently forgotten.

What are we, boxers? Let's look at rehearsals, for example. A fight! And hopeless, really, because they never schedule enough of them! And what's worse, they simply break the rehearsals off once they've gone past the allotted time, because the almighty union dictates what work hours are reasonable for musicians. First they start whispering, tapping on their watches, gesturing toward the conductor, who soon breaks off. Till tomorrow, then, gentlemen! One more handshake and you have yourself driven back to the hotel, you ride up to about the eight hundredth floor, walk down long corridors and end up at the end, at the end of another day, left in the end with only the desire to sleep, back in a room whose windows can't be opened. You should grab something heavy and just smash the panes! Isn't there a user's manual anywhere around here?

What an amazingly rare specimen, this man. He represents hope, which drives all the young cellists to him, even the very young, who come to him led on the hand of a sister, mother, or father; they all want to be his student, to learn from him, be taught by him. He seems to have held on to something that most people lose over the course of their lives. He is truly hunting music as if working out some secret, in search of the pure sound of truth. He manages to create the magic that occurs only when tinder and tenderness mix.

But what am I doing talking big to you, my dear Suvorin. This here, on the other hand, he says—and all of a sudden his voice sounds soft and gentle again—this sublime game with its balls, beyond all vulgarity, is no prison. And the clack of the balls in the stillness of a late hour is the only sound that can still be taken seriously after a concert.

And if there was also a fire burning in the hearth, all the better. And he, surprisingly enough, given how rarely I visit, also remembered my fondness for chocolate—and spoiled me with the finest pralines.

He took a ball, sent it rolling and—*clack!*—it softly hit another. It's all so precious, the perfect expression of something distant, infinite!

He loved the cello, Beethoven, even if he didn't write a single concerto for it. Five piano concertos! Not one for cello, his great love.

Schiff has played the sonatas for cello and piano, and nods. The Triple Concerto, too, where this love for the cello reaches its full bloom. The piano is responsible for tempo and rhythm. The piano is the chaperone, in a way. The cello, on the other hand, gets to play, it's the child whom everything is permitted, leaping, dancing, and on top of it all, singing.

Exactly! That's what I always preached to my piano students. When you play the Piano Trio, everything proceeds from the cello.

And then he goes and writes a concerto for the violin. Ugh!

Out of bashfulness? I've often asked myself that. Was Beethoven bashful? No one puts what he loves out there for all to see. Beethoven, who wears himself out as a composer, but doesn't abandon himself. True love was abstention. Therefore, something as monumental as a cello concerto was out of the question. You don't tip your hand. His devotion remained intimate. You long for everything from love, true, but the fact is, you don't expect a thing from it, and certainly not *everything*.

Schiff was amused at how I couldn't stop inscribing the trait of love for the cello—which of course wasn't even my instrument—into the psychological profile of this man whom everyone believes they know everything about. He calmly accepted the fact that a concerto that hadn't been composed did not exist. There were, he thought, plenty of others. But he seemed surprised that a pianist of all people would seem so inconsolable about it. Should he ask the reasons for this? Maybe the memory of someone who played the cello, loved Beethoven and couldn't get enough of loving him. Had they perhaps exchanged letters about it, developed certain theories, maybe fought over whether as a musician you trust your ear or your soul?

Ah, yes. Schiff, I knew, had always been suspicious of these all too delicate souls and their sensitivity, had seen them as tiresome and as a danger for musical practice. Besides that, they gave him a headache.

Why was it, actually, it occurred to me, almost incidentally— why had it never happened that the two of us, he and I, neither publicly nor in private, had ever played music together?

The cello was his secret, his secret weapon. A secret code. Beethoven encrypted what he couldn't say, especially not to a woman; but he couldn't keep silent on the matter either. The only consequences to devolve from his beautiful, tender confessions were musical in nature. And music was something he knew a thing or two about. Music was interesting. Music he had a handle on.

Schiff had never much concerned himself with claims that,

even if they weren't stupid, still couldn't be proven. What took the vigor out of every thought he could have given himself over to was the pain in his shoulder, this lousy pain—next to this sting of Satan's the soul was nothing but a tired old philosopher. *Lousy* isn't even the expression for it, snorted Schiff. Where's the Holy Spirit that's supposed to knead me back to health? Even if it does it just for the music's sake. But no! Not even the doctors have it under control, not a single one I've consulted. Good show, gentlemen!

I thought of old Schwarzberg, who also has trouble with her shoulder, has had it for a long time now, but makes a point of never mentioning it, nor indeed does she mention the man she puts all her hope in and whose business card she gave me once, with some sesquipedalian name on it, I assume it's Indian or Nepalese, I must have it lying around somewhere in the mess I have at home. No, not a word. If you can't at least be alone with your pain in this world, you'll feel even more lost.

I think it was more than fine with him that I didn't pity him, that his bad mood didn't shut me up. Someone who writes a letter, I said, waits for an answer. Not music. Music doesn't wait—and doesn't expect anything. In the end Beethoven didn't even expect approval for what he composed.

I was talking like someone who was lost in his own drunken thoughts, but I was only drinking tap water, even back then, much to the chagrin of my host. It was red wine for him, at a temperature of exactly sixteen degrees Celsius, he was stubborn about that. He could get into an argument with any waiter at any restaurant—and with the manager, too, if he had to. I never experienced it myself, but heard tell from others. A meal with him, if they're to be believed, can't have been an enjoyable experience. He was livid. In every show of friendliness from a waiter, he sensed haughtiness, as if he, the customer, should consider it an honor just to be noticed by the staff. He sized up the other customers at the neighboring tables with disapproval. Nothing about them escaped his criticism. They were all too loud, too rich, too uncultivated. And yet another thing he would have his way about: the bottle, which, after all, he was paying for, belonged next to the plates and not over on a little table out of reach.

What is the cloth merchant doing in our story, anyway? I don't like that noble gentleman either. You? That leaves his carpenter, who of course was an artist, a master of his trade, a man with a firm grip on the essentials in life. Everything sleeps within the wood, says music. All feeling is equation, says mathematics. Everyone be quiet for a moment, says poetry. I would dig him out of the earth with my own two hands—he sets down the glass, which has been empty for some time, and holds them up toward me—if that would bring him back to life.

You don't have to sit in some club in England somewhere with cigar-smoking, gin-drinking old gentlemen, or in Leipzig, in the thick air of a philosophical seminar, to find enjoyment in conversations of this sort. There is little that is more seductive than beauty, handed down in the mythology of particular objects, a violin or a cello, an antique pool table—or a well-bound book, with beautiful type set on beautiful paper.

Maybe that explains the presence of so many books in his apartment—works of literature mostly, but also science books. Books in bookcases, tables loaded with books, stacks of them, a proper library, it's enough to make you feel ashamed. The last person he had thrown out of his apartment was someone who wanted to know if he'd read all of them. An idiot.

I heard him sigh. Nowhere are there so many idiots as you get among lovers of music. A milieu that can wear you down.

Their thinking only goes halfway. They're content with half a life. For reasons that are inexplicable, they completely refuse to see life as something alive. Plus, and this is even worse, they feel themselves superior to all life, everything living, the cheerfulness of everything living. There's no helping them. There's something oppressive about it, like in a bad dream when you lose your way and everything gets dark. What could you possibly have done to bring yourself to this point? For what did you learn everything there was to be learned? Why let yourself in for an unhappy life just because you're a musician?

But what a happy life, too! He didn't like to make a show of it, but: a life close to the flame! Suvorin remembered a comment that a writer, a friend of Schiff's, had once made about him. To get so close to the flame that a bonfire envelops you.

He had given Suvorin a ride back to the city from a suburb outside Vienna, where young people had played chamber music and the old man hadn't been above helping out as a page turner, and on the way they had started up a conversation. The light from a bonfire is all it takes. Light of that unmistakable quality that emanates into the world from the people they call geniuses. Suvorin's face darkened. He didn't like the word genius. It was propaganda. There were intellectual endeavors for which other talents were necessary than a well-functioning brain, quick fingers, a sense for color. What emanates from a woman who, as she nestles up against someone, manages to think of nothing other than nothing? A person who loves doesn't think of love. No? Are you sure of that? Suvorin goes quiet. Had he said that, or was it his friendly chauffeur, who would do better to stop thinking about love, because a sudden downpour had just come on? A dangerously beautiful music, as it happens, a kind of small apocalypse. But, unlike the two of them now, you're not always sitting somewhere safe and dry when it all comes crashing down.

Suvorin smoothed the tablecloth, as billiard players do with the green baize before a game, a reverent, circumspect, elegant gesture, closer to a caress than a practical consideration. I should get moving. A short walk, and then I'm there.

XVI

EVER TRIED CARAMELIZED

ONIONS?

The question caught Suvorin off guard. And Schiff could tell.

Poor people have always found things to do with onions. Until one day the gourmets got interested in them. I got interested, too, after the first attempt I made. Little work, big results. Where else can you be so greatly rewarded for minuscule effort and as good as no cost?

He grew quite lively all of a sudden. I'd be happy to write the recipe down for you, if you want. All very simple. You take a pot, not too big, and put butter in it. Then sugar. Brown them very slightly. Place the onions in the pot, whole. Peeled, of course. Let them cook gently for ten minutes. Then, very important, pour red wine over the onions till they're half covered. Put the lid on and let them simmer on low heat for twenty minutes. Finally, reduce the red wine so that just a little sauce is left over on the bottom. And you're done!

Schiff looked at me. And then at his cell phone, which was ringing. For the tenth time, he turned it off without even checking to see who had tried to reach him. Yesterday I had a visit from Leonskaja, "I was going for a walk and I passed by your place," she said—actually she lives nowhere near here, but still I was pleased. What an old girl she is, but a girl who's never grown old, a creature with the warmth of a child in her heart. She gave off an air of gentle resignation, as if she had stopped believing in the moment when she would meet a man, probably a much younger man, and fall in love again. She doesn't even want to read stories like that in novels, she said. The shame of having to come to grips with the ridiculousness of a late love affair. Being hurt by friends' goodwill in trying to act understanding. Hurting herself with the fear of no longer being able to handle the happiness, were it to come her way once more. Accepting that she has now lived twice as long as someone like Franz Schubert, if not more. I don't want to sleep anymore, because I don't want to have the face I wake up with. What, dear merciful God, do you do to fight the bags under your eyes? It almost hurts to be admired, if what you want is more than admiration. How lonely it is around her, how lonely around us all. How to live with the knowledge that it's all behind you? To be gentle, and tender, and both with enthusiasm! I could see it, looking at her, as she sat across from me, even if it was barely there: the last glimmer of hope, waiting for a miracle that was no longer very likely. A glance at a window covered with frost!

Schiff went looking for a cigarette, found one, and lit it. I tried of course to cheer her up with compliments, but she just smiled. It seems like something, maybe the most important thing in the life of a woman, is gone for good, and she knows it. Uses music to cling to life, and with success. She's still got it, the doll, you have to hand it to her! But of course, you know her, she can't help talking about Richter, her Richter, her dear friend and teacher, which is of course a kind of homesickness, if not despair, and hearing her you just don't know what to say.

A moment of silence ensued. Really, what can you say? Is she looking for solace among the dead? Was there something else to it? I mean, was it one of these insane fits of passion that still, even now, gets her into such a state?

And again Schiff stopped speaking for a moment. He seemed to have caught the trail of some thought or another and wanted to find the right words, the right tone. It's funny, really, that as a musician who plays classical music it's a mortal sin to want to be original, but that, on the other hand, it can be tedious if a person who is of course admired as an artist stops producing anything original, even if it's just a hint of something in conversation, a gesture, a surprising insight, a thought that, even if it doesn't lead to anything, at least shines brightly for a brief moment. Here I am, says the light, look at me, look at yourselves, wait for me in the darkness. Don't wait, however, for something like enlightenment when I return. Why is it that we, unlike any scientist in any laboratory, aren't allowed to make mistakes? What does that do to us? Not a single wrong note! Everything flawless, clean, and beautiful. When I performed I sometimes had an overwhelming desire to play like a pig. Not so overbred. Schiff was speaking without any inhibition now, beads of sweat on his forehead, his hands restless, his body tense in the same way it was when he was bent over his instrument. Concerning the artist as "cultural product"! What about what we do is irrefutable? I've never gotten to the bottom of it. Where did it all begin, and how could we get back to that point?

Schiff shuddered. Someone who wants to please has no business on a stage. Nor does anyone who doesn't at least suggest to the audience that its presence might be less than desired. Keep up the struggle, doll, I said to her. I think she was just about to start crying. And, to be honest, so was I.

When the time comes, thought Suvorin, a little spoonful of earth for you, too, Lisa. Contrary to how Schiff saw things, however, the last time he saw her she hadn't given him the impression that her troubles were all that serious. Still has it all under control, as they say. But please, I'm no expert at seeing what goes on inside another person. Suvorin trusted what he saw, wouldn't take any bets on what remained unseen. What a grand, formidable sight she is, even today, no question about that. When she performs she still has such energy, there's not the least sign of flagging, and on top of that—and this much he had been struck by forty years ago in Moscow—there's her full head of hair, which she still has today and which makes her so stunning! She doesn't seem to be in a hurry to cede the spotlight to the new crop, and that without any misplaced ambition. Let them settle their beauty contests among themselves. She doesn't struggle, she lets what she does happen. She's no ally of any record company, she allies herself with composers— develops or, better yet, renews friendships with them. Her execution is commanding. Nothing about it is stale, historical. Whoever wants to conquer the new millennium, let them. She digs into the depths. That's right, they do still exist! Discoveries that you make with steady patience, not by barreling ahead and not with bravura. No reason to worry, then, Suvorin thought, but to argue with Schiff he felt would have been inappropriate, and also useless. He had no need to feel he had the upper hand, just because he—like she—was Russian. On top of that was the fact that this stubborn bastard here was simply too intelligent for him, and most certainly less sentimental. A man of sorrows, but ready to strike, like a wounded animal. And of course maybe someone whose strength is leaving him actually does see deeper into another's soul.

After she was gone, two of my students stopped in whom I spoiled, as I had Lisa before them, with my by-then-completely-drunken onions. He himself had to laugh about it. Naturally I didn't tell them anything about "little work, big results"!

He sat up in his chair and gestured behind him with a motion of his head. There's still a bit left on the stove. Tastes good cold, too. How about it? Hungry?

No, thank you. Another time, though, I'd be happy to. Very happy even.

Schiff gave up trying to convince me to at least have a taste. If I know you Russians, you'd rather just eat the things raw.

Schiff's apartment didn't look as though he had a constant stream of visitors. He could barely even stand having a maid around.

XVII

ENOUGH SALT?

Heinrich Schiff died a few weeks ago, and Suvorin is thinking about the pool table in his apartment.

And when he thinks of the pool table, he thinks of Mozart.

He can imagine Schubert at a tavern. He can imagine Beethoven at his desk. But neither of them at a pool table.

Mozart, yes, he had one when things were going well for him.

He even had a horse, when things were going well for him.

Schiff had, Suvorin couldn't begin to believe it, a Rolls-Royce, and Suvorin envied him more for having the nerve for such extravagance than for the car itself.

He also envied him his pool table.

I can imagine the two of them playing pool. Mozart rides home afterward.

Schiff I can't imagine on a horse. I can imagine him holding the reins in his hand, but not the horse.

With Mozart I can imagine the horse, but not him holding the reins. Not even in his marriage was he holding the reins.

It was probably the case that Mozart had hardly opened his eyes when he started seeing black spots everywhere. And making music out of them.

Grown older, he made music out of color. Out of color, a heaven. What other explanation is there?

If fairy tales, as they should, outdo even themselves in improbability, then the two of them, Mozart and Schiff, are with us still, and not just in heaven.

But it's not just fairy tales that offer the improbable, even the much-maligned everyday reality of our lives sometimes shows some nerve, because Heinrich Schiff's last address when he was alive was: 1040 Vienna, Mozartgasse 4.

An address like you'd find in a penny dreadful, as he, amused, would on occasion proclaim. The only thing missing is a plaque on the building's facade, a chocolate one, put there just for me.

You really envied him for his Rolls-Royce?

Why do you ask? Does it surprise you?

To be honest, yes.

When I was a child I envied people who got on trains, long-distance trains. Whenever I earned a treat and was allowed to ask for something, it was to get to go to the train station, to see the people, watch them as they waited for their trains, waited to depart on some big, long journey. If I was lucky, there it was, the train I had secretly been hoping for. I owned a toy version of it, which no one other than me was allowed to touch. What the Rolls-Royce is among cars, the gleaming carriages of the Compagnie Internationale des Wagons-Lits et des Grands Express Européens were among trains, all lined up in a row, each car bearing a golden inscription, a moving grand hotel, the staff wore white gloves; I could see through the windows as they, like dolls, set the tables in the restaurant car. Lights glowed in the sleeper cars. Curtains were drawn. At a respectful distance I walked past it, up and down, and my thoughts carried me away. And my heart pounded! I—

Suvorin broke off.

That's how it is, you see? You have dreams. You never leave childhood completely. I even asked Schiff, years ago, when we happened to see each other at a music festival somewhere in Burgenland, who it was he was planning on leaving the limousine to in his will.

The good Lord, he answered.

And that's about how he played, too, as I sat in the crowd at the church—for God, which usually only Russians can do, as though he were playing out of sheer love for Him, in wild, reckless ecstasy. Like someone who doesn't believe in the Almighty, strictly speaking, but who wants to come to an understanding with Him, wants to make peace with Him. If only every nonbeliever would make the effort!

The effect?

Unfathomable achievement.

And now he's dead!

That he is, there's no denying it. I can't even bring him back the books I borrowed.

And no more pool either.

He cooked, the last time I visited him, hoping for a game of pool—who would have thought that it really would be the last time—he cooked soup, good, nourishing, tasty soup, as it turned out. He invited me to share his table.

He was no longer healthy. It was more than just a run of bad luck, health-wise. This time, he felt, was different.

Death is at work within me, he said.

It does that, sooner or later, in every one of us, one of his doctors had told him, but had asked Schiff to try to stay alive a little longer.

On that point, Schiff was—undecided.

It's a question of will, the doctor said.

It's a question of wanting to, Schiff retorted.

In the end, a question of the heart.

Whether it's healthy enough to be able to think clearly.

Those were good conversations. Not all of them, not with every doctor. Not all of them knew the importance of humor. Truth unleashes confusion, which, if it persists, spills over into lies.

As it turned out, Schiff had the habit of writing notes to himself, a not unusual activity for such a dedicated reader as he. And popping up again and again among the notes are quotes that were clearly important to him, taken from books by all manner of authors—from Schiller ("Its goal is at one with the very highest for which man has to struggle, to be free of passion, to look always clearly, always calmly around him and into himself, to find everywhere more chance than fate and to laugh more over absurdity than to rage or to weep over malice") to Puccini ("An invitation to a dinner makes me sick for a week"). He also noted, among other things, that he had consulted so many doctors, physical therapists, and massage therapists by this point that he could fill the Wiener Konzerthaus's Mozart-Saal with them. It grew and grew, the number of them working their "witchcraft" on him.

He didn't look like he enjoyed the thought of having to endure pain, the thought that soon he wouldn't be able to walk anymore, would barely be able to sit, that he might not even be able to lie down anymore, or to stand up without some stranger's help; already now he was unable to fall asleep, to say nothing of sleeping through the night, even one night. What was the point of this? What was he to do to counter the hostility that his body was mobilizing against him? How cannily, how stubbornly was he supposed to resist it? And the agonizing, at root unanswerable questions he asked himself when he lay awake at night. How much of his fate was his own fault, how much could be blamed on the mistakes he had made? If I lie in the wrong position at night, he said, I'm crippled. Every rib hurts, every breath. I can barely get up. Bend down to tie my shoes? Impossible! It takes such force of will just to blow my nose! Before the pain comes I feel it spreading down into my legs, my muscles, my temples. I feel the pain in my eyes and want nothing more than to tear them out. I see flashes of lightning. I'm buying eye drops for lightning flashes. I'm a customer at several pharmacies, a good customer. So he wrote in his notebooks. What did me in, he writes in another, what did me in as a musician was the never-diminishing pain in my shoulders, especially my right shoulder, the most crucial one for a cellist. That time I took a fall in that fancy hotel in Bucharest, that's when it started. One second of carelessness! A good mood and a daring dance step on my way down the stairs to a small festive reception. And boom! Headfirst! Reflexes taking over instantly: protect your hands, not your head. Protect the instrument, not the performer. When he picked himself up after his crash landing, those who had seen him in concert and had just now been applauding him in recognition of his performance directed their concern not toward him, no, but rather toward his instrument, which—unlike him—lay there unharmed, in its case, velvet-padded and insured for millions.

The doctor—this he remembered—who at his request had come to the hotel that night and examined him, had diagnosed a mild stroke as the cause and advised him to have his heart and kidneys checked in Vienna.

Anything but that, he thought, but after his return had resolved to draw up a will. He'd been planning to do it for years.

It was harder and harder for him to look after himself.

It was harder and harder for him not to weep when he was alone. And this was hard to bear. He'd always had a strong aversion toward people who couldn't keep themselves in check when it came to tears. But there was just this feeling—and this was new, and he was powerless against it—this feeling of his forsakenness, a vision of damnation. What a sight, if you could have seen him. A man with tears running down his cheeks, who nevertheless forbids himself to feel any sympathy for the situation.

We suffer as penance for being alive—he wrote this! What else do I have left to give?

This is followed by a list, drawn up by him in pencil in fairly ornate handwriting and running clear across an otherwise empty page, a kind of ranking system, with names and numbers, the names of cellists with their final tally of years: Casals 96 years, Starker 88 years, Baldovino 82 years, Rostropovich 80 years, Fournier 79 years, Mainardi 78 years, Tortelier 76 years, Piatigorsky 73 years . . .

A comment referring to this list comes a few pages later and reads: me (63), limited mobility, swollen joints, difficulty breathing, dizzy spells. A man haunted by dreams of how it feels to be young and strong. I will make it happen. I will climb the mountain. I will lead my students to the summit. I wish I . . . (The rest illegible, crossed out with a thick pencil!) No more final definitive recording of the six cello suites! No more sending the bow dancing over the strings. So nothing at all anymore! So . . . (Line breaks off.)

Thus writes a man from whom everything that makes up a life has been taken.

A page later the following short note: Not even my thoughts move how I want them to. They obey me only if I concentrate on the pencil I use to write them down.

Was he, sitting there with his bowl of soup in front of him—was he thinking about suicide?

Once, said Suvorin, as I was looking for the bathroom in his apartment, the dimensions of which I could never really grasp, I got completely lost and ended up in a room that clearly had been set up as an office at some point, and maybe was still being used as one, but which seemed abandoned. You certainly couldn't have spoken of an ambitious drive to maintain order, not from the way it looked in there. Right away, I felt completely at home. That's how it looks throughout my entire apartment, like the offices of a company that's gone bankrupt. Letters, contracts, papers, books, sheet music. On the windowsill a vase with dried lilac stems, a clothes iron, and a cookie tin. In the corners there were rolled-up posters in packing paper. In a basket next to the door—like something that's waiting to be taken to the laundromat—shirts, socks, sweaters, a red baseball cap. Lying across an open laptop a case for a bow that was God knows where. The telephone—there had to have been one—hidden, maybe impossible to unearth. By one of the windows an exercise bike, on its seat a bag of flower bulbs. A silk scarf was draped over a chair, the only one someone could have sat down to do work in; the other three were reserved for all sorts of printed matter: concert programs, magazines, journals, newspapers. Hadn't he said one time that he kept a secretary? If that was the case, she must have taken the quote by Voltaire that was written in all caps and pinned to one of the walls as an injunction and forgotten her scarf in her haste as she left, giving herself the brief remainder of her earthly life off—a quote that read: "We have but three days on this earth, let us enjoy them!"

An insight which, unlike his secretary (if there ever was one!), someone like Schiff was up in arms against, without knowing it himself. He could lose all self-control and unleash a barrage of hair-raisingly obscene curses, the kind you usually save for the dentist when he comes at you with a syringe. He felt better immediately afterward, though, which had something touching about it. You almost wanted to put your arms around him—only who would ever have dared do so!—like the fine, dear man that at heart of course he was. In our language there's an expression for people like him, which sounds hard but is meant with warmth and affection. We say they're *packed in ice*. He was one of them. A person with a good heart, but unapproachable, on guard against intimacy and contact.

Like I said, he filled page after page, by hand. Whatever he felt like writing. Some notes dated, others not. Some pages covered in writing, others with just a bit of text. I'm walking with a cane, stands written there, the words framed by a circle that a glass of red wine left on the page. Even needed assistance to go out onstage for the first time. Was that a whisper that went through the hall? Was I the only one to hear it because I was imagining it? Is a life lived between cane and conductor's baton still a life at all? The limits of a life, of my life? The sadly oppressive feeling of having outlived myself. There was once a river that flowed through a man. And today: a river that flows only on Sundays. And then there are sentences or fragments of sentences. The eyes of my instrument! Breathing against fear. It is thinking that makes us mortal. Under it a doodle, crude, but unmistakably Chaplin, the little man with the cane. He stumbles, but doesn't fall. And if he falls, he gets back up. Not all the stories were through telling.

Suvorin savored it.

Enough salt?

Enough!

Schiff seemed not to have an appetite, he hadn't even tried the soup. Instead of eating, he played with the specks of oil in his bowl. He pushed them this way and that with the tip of his spoon. Maybe they formed a pattern that pleased him.

Ever sat in a Rolls-Royce before?

I took that as a compliment, a big compliment. Clearly he didn't think it beneath the dignity of an old, modest-minded Russian to have once succumbed to the temptation to make himself comfortable in such a magisterial automobile, maybe even behind the wheel.

Do you even have a driver's license? Tolstoy didn't have one, far as I know.

No, probably not.

The Rolls sits in the garage on Attersee most of the year, he said. In Vienna it would be ridiculous. People would think I'm a snob. Me! Not even my friends in London managed to make one of me, back when I was living there, and they tried everything. They tried to drag me to their tailors, their shoemakers and shirtmakers. The finest cloth, the finest leather! World-class workmanship! A golden opportunity! It was grand to hear all of this, even to believe it, but to have myself measured, freshly outfitted, and—I had to sit and listen to this, too—have them turn me into an elegant gentleman? Were they joking? I thought. Are they nuts? To allow myself to be teased by a men's clothing salesman who's telling me the symmetry of my shoulders left something to be desired? To have to hear a cobbler who had been elevated to the peerage by the Queen herself tell me in a courtly drawl that I had problematic feet, after which I might also have to receive a lecture on "the healthy way to walk on two legs," with the suggestion that either I see an orthopedist as soon as possible or I start hypnosis treatment? To have a shirtmaker look me up and down and then advise me in flawless Oxford English to watch my weight? No thanks. Fish and sausages for breakfast, that was fine, though it took some effort, but that's where I drew the line. That I finally went and bought that tub was, I think, a kind of self-defense. Somehow I had the feeling I had to placate them, and it worked, too. They appreciated my high regard for British culture. This was sufficient in their eyes. They forgave me.

The luster of supreme satisfaction flitted over his face.

What I need now is a cigarette. His third in a short span of time. Care for one, too?

Well, sure, why not, although . . .

I know, I know. Eventually everything is forbidden except dying. Here!

We smoked and were silent for a while.

Really I never wasted even a second on seriously trying to quit cigarettes. I suppose it's one of my gifts, never letting anyone tell me a thing where my personal life is concerned. Also where my health is concerned. When it comes to music, gladly. But please, no well-meaning bits of advice! I don't work that way. They still took me to task, the people closest to me—the only ones I'd even listen to. For God's sake, Heinrich, this awful scruffy beard on your face, it's not distinguished looking, it's disfiguring. Some of them didn't call it a beard, they called it undergrowth. Has no one ever told you what it makes you look like? The whole speech of course set off with a look of authentic concern. Keep going, I said, what else you got, what else do you need to get off your chest? Heinrich, please, don't set foot onstage with that idiotic red bow tie again, really. Well why not? In England people love it, in South Africa, too. Because it spoils the whole pleasure of your performance for people, and they, okay, I can't stop staring at the dumb thing. You look like a cheap emcee, when in fact you're one of the handful of cello virtuosos still left in the world. My last birthday, even though this is all well in the past and my performing days are over and done with, still brought a bounty of seven neckties. I thought of Schiller and said my thank-yous. Bah! I'd rather not even be seen. What were they criticizing me for? Did they think I was putting on a costume?

He was reminded of it whenever his agent asked him for new headshots for this concert or that poster, this program or that recording. His anger at his appearance, the impossibility of doing without a face at all. He simply didn't like himself in photos. And he didn't like the photographers either. They acted like they were granting him an audience. Like they were giving him permission to witness something extraordinary. It's best if you look up, sort of off into the distance a bit. And act natural! How do you do that, exactly, act natural as you stare off into the beyond? And don't tense up. We can take a break, if you like. Only thing missing was them asking you if there was any beer in the fridge. For a time he insisted on female photographers. He could be charming. He was hoping that something might come of the attitude he assumed around members of the opposite sex. He made them the focus of attention, which took the pressure off him. He was clever at distracting himself with thoughts concerning the lives of these women, who at the end of the day were doing a job, who came dressed casually, more or less attractive, but at least none of them were exaggeratedly done up, hardly any wore makeup. The ones who looked a bit out of sorts were the ones he liked best. An idiot of a husband, a painful divorce, a new boyfriend, no new boyfriend, rainy weather, a drink or two here and there, a difficult kid, maybe two, in every life there accrued certain things that he could use to occupy his thoughts, so much so that he completely forgot what was actually happening. Oh right, new photos. Horrible! I have to put an end to that. Never again in my life do I want to be caught on film. There had been times when he had called sessions off, even ones with female photographers. The friendliest thing he could be bothered to leave his victims with was a remark like "You're wasting my time" or "I'll call you when I'm feeling more photogenic."

He could also take a completely different approach, however, and ask the person getting ready to examine him from behind the lens of her camera, with utter bewilderment: What's that you're doing, exactly? Me? Yes, you. I'm photographing you. Oh, is that so? And why is that? Because I'm a photographer. And you make a living from it? What do you make for a job like this? And she would think about it for a while and then name a sum. And then Schiff would go looking for his wallet, take a few bills out, and hand them to her. Here. And that's enough for today!

Lately his agent was asking for portraits of him in color.

And then there's "my behavior," which I know a few people don't appreciate. Okay, it could well have happened that when I was at some reception, before they had officially opened it up, I might have reached out and grabbed something from the buffet, a sandwich, a sausage, a piece of cake, and then ignored the waiter who tried to force a fork and napkin on me. It may well be that once or twice, good God, I stuck my finger in a bowl of goulash, just to taste it. What's it matter? I was hungry, you get hungry after work. I felt like it. And so long as I had my mouth full, I didn't have to answer any questions. Did I have perfect pitch. Did I, from a musical standpoint, prefer the nineteenth century to the twentieth. Who did I consider the greatest living cellist. Was there anything to the rumor that I'd bought one of Queen Elizabeth II's Rolls-Royces. I had just discovered the platter of roast beef, so sorry, don't have the time. I didn't buy it, she gave it to me!

His laugh, louder than might be considered polite, demonstrated his thoroughgoing aversion to all these things that people were so fascinated by, even right after a concert.

I am old-fashioned and behave like a completely normal person. Rarely does this elicit delight. That's just how he is, said the bravest of my friends. Yes, that's how I am. How I was, I should say. I had to feel that I was alive. That was my weapon, I'll admit it, that's what I had at my disposal. Why act like a genius bored with his success? When I gave a concert, so long as my mother still recognized me as her son, I was fine with things. She was the only person who got to pass judgment on my character. She knew all about me always sticking my finger in the cooking pot. She didn't like how impatient I could be, but that I always had an appetite, that she did like.

It completely escaped his notice that he'd smoked his cigarette down to the filter, and when he did notice he threw the butt in the ashtray. He pushed the dish of ginger candies toward me and helped himself from another, the one with the olives in it. Over there, you see them, the pipes? Tried it once, that was enough. Waste of money. Take the time for a cigar? Maybe. Later. Sometime. Smug bunch. To smoke a good cigar—I hear somebody say that and I'm done. Who would want to smoke a bad one? Who would want to play a cello that produces sounds like the floorboards in the room Schubert died in?

One more thing about my fancy car, Suvorin, even if you're going to think I'm superstitious. I found it out as I was signing the papers, with, what else, a cup of tea in my hand. The date my new friend was first registered was November 18, my birthday.

Suvorin looked at me. I think, he said, that there was another reason for his refusing to let himself be dressed up, a very personal one, almost tragic in its dimensions. He—and he would hardly be an exception in this—didn't handle comments about his body well; he was offended by them. You can tell whether it comes easily to a person—or indeed, whether it comes hard—to feel secure in his own skin. With him, though, I had the feeling that there was something else at work, and not just when the pain started, and the operations which he always had a hard time agreeing to caused him to lose all confidence in his doctors, and with it, in fact, all hope of recovery: with him there was a, how should I put it, an almost spiteful indifference to his own health. He didn't love his body, and maybe that's how he wanted it. Maybe I shouldn't say that. I didn't know him well enough. But then again, I haven't met anyone who would claim to have known him. Was there a woman in his life? Did he have friends, people he couldn't live without? Who knows? It always seemed to me that instead of having to be a ball, he wanted to be a dart. But at bottom he was a peasant like me, someone with the build of a peasant, the bones of a peasant, a man with a plain, lucid mind. He was no romantic, that's for sure. Back home we have an expression that he makes me think of: *When a man like him walks across a field, you feel sorry for the flowers.* You understand? He sweated like a peasant, too. I don't think he liked that. As if the sweat that poured off him gave something away.

But now his skin was dry, his face pale, and the glasses on his nose were crooked, because one of the earpieces had broken off. The bags under his eyes, tinged with blue, amplified the impression of a profound, incurable weariness.

Finally, after several minutes lost in thought, Schiff turned his attention to the soup in front of him, dipped the spoon in, waited for it to stop dripping, lifted it to his mouth.

As I'm sure you know, Joyce was blind, or as good as. The canton police never allowed him to drive, never in his life. Plus, of course, he was rarely sober. Seems he couldn't handle much liquor. And what could have interested him about driving? The intoxication of speed, maybe?

Joyce? Hadn't Schiff just been speaking about Tolstoy? Hadn't he just asked him if Tolstoy had had a driver's license?

He would have had to hold on to that hat he always wore.

The spoon still hovered in midair.

Did you cook this?

What?

The soup.

Oh, right, the soup. Yes. My winter soup. You'll spill it all over yourself if you're not careful. To be on the safe side, he put the spoon back in the bowl, still full. Come visit me sometime if you're ever in the Salzkammergut. We'll go for a drive.

Suvorin sees him still, leaning against the Rolls-Royce, his instrument, a Stradivarius cello, stowed away in the trunk, in his hand a thermos of green tea that he's already drunk half of. It was a hot day, and he had been sweating, like he always did whenever he exerted himself. Now he was looking forward, he said, to the drive home, windows down. And to being able to be by himself for a while, to not speak, to just be quiet, just tired, just completely out of it, rolling along slowly on small roads, without having to apologize.

This confection of an automobile—a Silver Cloud II, built in 1959, one of the first models of the new series begun just that year, a product of the highest imaginable manufacturing standard—seemed to have been made for precisely this, for brief moments of movement in the slowly dwindling light of day. As if in an attempt at enchantment, the twilight would come, and with it thoughts, neither new nor old nor originating in the hollow of a skull. He would drive into a wide-open infinity that shielded him on all sides.

The engine was scarcely to be heard, which had been a chief reason behind the decision to buy a Rolls, just a gentle, quiet, confidence-inspiring rumble that bothered no one when you drove through the countryside, neither hikers nor bicyclists, not rabbits, not deer, not even the driver. Engine noise of "high musical quality," as Schiff said. It was moments like this, moods like this, that moved him to think, with the same reverence he had always felt for the masters of Cremona and Venice, of the men who'd had a hand in the construction of this automobile, of the engineers and technicians, of all the fine nameless fellows in the factories! Were there doctors out there who, with similar skill, might be able to do something for him, who, with their knowledge, might still be able to help him?

Of course there was no helping him. He had given enough proof, all throughout his life, of how good he was at hurting himself.

He thought he had the car key in his hand, thought he felt its weight, but no, nothing doing. With a car this size you can almost get in standing up, a ceremony, a royal pleasure, however you might look at it—but what to do without the key?

He patted his jacket, his shirt. Then a smile. It lay in the gravel at his feet. You have to stoop down after all.

XVIII

CAN YOU MAKE GOD LAUGH?

I was curious. A woman like you find at the circus. A thoroughbred of a violinist, a genius of a teacher. In both respects a natural talent. Always on the go, when she's not sitting in her sumptuously upholstered chair in her apartment in Vienna, in her salon, her violin ever within reach. A sight worth seeing, whatever the case. Say I'm in New York, she says, fending someone off when her friend or a student picks up the phone. I'm not here, end of story. Although she was at home, you were more likely to hear that she was at that very moment teaching in Turin.

Wherever she lived, they remembered her. Wherever she performed, they longed for her next concert. A professor for years, and, all in all, no longer in great health. But I don't know a single healthy person who exudes such liveliness. You'll get to know her eventually, I'm sure. It's unavoidable. Who can stay hidden in Vienna? To run into someone, you don't even have to leave the house. I'll tell you what you have to know. An exact physical description, so to speak, thank you very much. No taller than a matchstick, round as a pipe bowl! He said it just as seriously as you might deliver an earnest compliment. Didn't those clever Greeks admire perfection in the form of the sphere? Back at the conservatory, her professor affectionately called her "B.B.," and sometimes, when he was particularly pleased with her, and because in everything she did she was calm as can be, "B.B. Buddha." The little Buddha! Aside from that he was generally inclined to pay her the most wonderful compliments, even well into old age. Schwarzberg, he remembered, she was famous before anybody even knew who she was! They could have strung her violin with barbed wire, she would still have been able to make music with it.

Suvorin also remembered. She was always a stand-out, a Jewish stand-out from Odessa, her hometown, she wouldn't hear anything said against it. When she was in a good mood, and when was she not, she liked to quote a line from the autobiography of Leonid Utyosov, who was born Lazar Weissbein and became a legend as "Sasha the Fiddler": "I was born in Odessa. You think I'm putting you on? But it's true. Lots of people would like to have been born in Odessa, but not everybody manages it!" Her kind of line! As his music was her kind of music, and the music of those who had learned from him. The old songs from Odessa. Forbidden songs, songs for people whom poverty had yet to deprive of their sense of humor. Pirated music, recorded on cheap cassettes and sold on the sly. She had it on her phone. She knew that all her life she would have to draw strength from the place of her birth. And so it hummed within her and hums to this day, the good, wild spirit of rebellion. I don't want to have to be dead while I'm still alive, she said, and packed her suitcases and her two violins. Always this damned fear! You can't train yourself not to have it. It starts with minor acts of impudence. With a grin on their faces. We'll see each other again, Miss, they tell you, which doesn't just sound like a threat, it is one. What to do? Wait till the transformation, till they turn you into a woman condemned? Always in the shadow of absolute power? But when you start to get offended, you're finished. How do you fight back? She imagined her departure and what she would tell the customs officer about her violins.

No, she wouldn't say it at all, she would hum it, that little song she liked. Yes, sir, that's my baby! And then add: Twins!

Can you make God laugh?

She tried to. She left. We all left.

My heart never stops being true to you, my wife declaring her love for the country to which she longed to return. Not me. I was through with it. I'd tip the first shoeshine boy I saw. And drink proper coffee. Buy myself a hat, light up a Chesterfield, and squint in the sun. And press my wife close to me, no matter where we were.

Long time ago, all of it. And over time, time itself grows long on you. It doesn't move as it once did. Sometimes fast, sometimes slowly, but always in motion. Today it seems like it doesn't know what to do anymore with an old man like me.

Suvorin ran a hand over his face. Maybe she's home now, wherever she is. He seemed to be reflecting on the power of believing in the efficacy of pious wishes, without any conviction that prayers could do any good. The holiness that was in her, he said, will help her.

His eyes shone with warmth. And a calm came over him.

And you, he asked before we parted, what do you believe in?

By the time we see each other again, I'll have thought it over, I said. And I hurried off.

I had agreed to meet with a man in the lobby of one of the big hotels on Vienna's Ringstraße, a man I knew only as a voice on the telephone, and I arrived to find him already waiting. An older gentleman, but fit looking, with bushy hair gone gray at the temples, the owner of a dog kennel, as it turned out, who got right to the point.

As you might remember, if you know your Austrian history, on September 10, 1898, the twenty-five-year-old anarchist Luigi

Lucheni stabbed the Austrian empress Elisabeth with a sharpened iron file on the lakeside promenade in Geneva; she died twenty minutes later. Twelve years after that, Lucheni, too, was dead, a case with certain inconsistencies that I'll tell you about some other time, if we come to do business together. I'd also be happy to tell you a bit about the autopsy results concerning his skull, or more specifically his brain, which underwent a scientific examination, such as it was, without their being able to find an answer to the question of whether you could recognize a predisposition toward criminality in abnormalities of the convolutions in the brain. The top of his skull was put back on, the head preserved in a glass container filled with formaldehyde. So far, so good.

I'd actually been in the mood for a melange, but this mood had somehow left me—and I hadn't even taken my coat off yet. A water, please. Still.

Still was also how I felt inside. The image of a head floating in murky liquid wasn't easy to digest. A glimpse into what abyss? And to tell the truth, the head of the empress wouldn't have interested me either. In order to at least say something, I asked him how he, the murderer, had met his death.

He hanged himself. And you still see it on his face, his last dying struggle. The mouth contorted in the throes of death. The eyes open wide, from the asphyxiation, the terror in them. That's how he looks at us. Looked at us, I should say, unfortunately. But first things first.

Unfazed, the man went on with what he had to say. The object came to Vienna at Austria's request in 1985, under strict secrecy, accompanied by the military attaché to the Austrian embassy in Bern. With the stipulation that it be neither publicly displayed nor exploited in any form of media. The specimen disappeared into a room in the Pathological-Anatomical Collection of the Naturhistorisches Museum. But there were rumors, there was interest. A glass jar containing the head of the immortal Sisi's murderer, you understand? Incidentally, the file that Lucheni used to stab the empress to death can also be found in Vienna, in the Museum of Forensic Medicine, but it's kept in a safe for fear of souvenir hunters.

The man savored his melange after stirring three heaping spoonfuls of sugar into it.

There was nothing about the man, aside from his unhealthy sugar intake, that I could have found repulsive. He had bright, cheerful eyes, a pleasant voice. Who wouldn't have handed their dog over to him for boarding, or, as he put it, for "individually catered care"? A vacation for your dog! as it said in the brochure.

Back to the skull, he said. I don't want to take up too much of your time. In order to settle the matter permanently and for good, it was decided in February 2000 to dispose of the object, that is, the head. It was laid to rest in the Central Cemetery in Vienna, in the so-called Anatomy Memorial, where the cadavers from the Anatomical Institute are also interred.

He leaned back, relaxed. So that was it, then, a story with an unfortunate empress traveling under an assumed name, a murder, a suicide, and the fear that the head of the murderer, the trophy, so to speak, could end up in the hands of a lunatic, could be stolen, purloined, absconded with. There's a market for it. Collectors of all things Sisi. Beauty and Death. A fairy tale with horror at its core. And this horror has a face! It exists, it is material. It has a name. And, don't forget, it has a date, too, on top of that. We even know the time, down to the exact minute, 1:38 p.m.

He placed his hand on the glass table as if on a document. It's history, contemporary history. As you can see, he said, I'm informed. Thoroughly familiar with the case.

I felt little desire to try to coax him into telling me what he was after, although it was clear to me that he hadn't asked me to meet for nothing. What was it you did before you started running a hotel for dogs?

Oh, everything you can imagine, and, admittedly, some things you can't. I was a cook in Canada, chief receptionist at a hotel in the South of France, after that a freelance photographer on the coast and, occasionally, in the winter months, a con man. Yeah, you know, getting acquainted with rich widows and other lonely ladies. It's no picnic, I'll tell you that.

What the man wouldn't have guessed was that, of all his occupations, that of con man interested me the most, and I told him so. I've always had the greatest respect for con men, especially the ones in novels and movies, and still do to this day. Respect for those of them with class, of course. Men whom I envy for many of their abilities. Not jacks-of-all-trades, but rather specialists. Men with a good memory and a half-dozen life stories they can summon up at will. Men gifted with an almost mathematically honed imagination. Not one of your cheap dime-a-dozen gigolos, who tends to be more of a thief, a liar, a swindler, a petty crook. Con men are cut from a different cloth. In order to be successful, they must meet a broad array of criteria. First of all, naturally, to be good-looking and know how to dress, how to carry and comport themselves. They have to be charming and, in an unassuming way, witty, they have to be good at repartee and, very important, know a thing or two about alcohol. How to hold their liquor. To be able to enjoy a sunset, that, too. To have patience with women. This is no hustle, no cheap ploy, it goes without saying. What else? They have to speak at least four languages. And be able to tell real pearls from fake. And be able to gauge the purity of gold at a glance. And be able to drive a car not only very fast but also very slowly. Posers don't have a chance at the level I'm talking about, no chance at all. Neither do men with bad teeth, incidentally. Do they still exist, con men?

I quickly went back to cooking, my true passion, he said. If you come visit me, and I hope you will, I'll cook for you. In fact, I implore you to come visit me. I have something that will be of interest to you, now that you know the story. Me, I wasn't so sure of that. I don't like dogs.

On the coast I didn't have much success as a gallant, he said, with one exception, a lady from Vienna, a divorced woman, a doctor by trade, and what a coincidence, she had eminent, more or less professional connections in the field of forensic medicine. Once I found this out the rest of our days, mine and hers, were set, since from that point forward my sole aim was to get her to believe she owed me a favor. She didn't make it hard for me, as I found out, to my relief, that same evening, an evening spent literally under a palm tree. A victim in need of sympathy and understanding, and therefore a grateful one. One confidence for another. In place of love, a deal.

If there were music, this is where the strings would come in. I waited.

I have more than a dozen pictures. I did it. I photographed him. I am in possession of the only extant records of the assassin's head! It was a race against time, since the date had already been set when he would vanish from view, for all of us, vanish even from the history of the monarchy, vanish for good.

Could he possibly believe he had rendered a service to his fatherland, maybe even to humanity?

And, pardon, but what do I have to do with it? I asked. Why are you telling me all this?

Because I want you to write about it. There are collectors, as I've said. It's a matter of finding them. It's a matter of making them aware. Could we do business together?

I'm going to put an end to this guy's charade, I thought, and felt pleased with myself. Enough, more than enough! No false confidences, anything but that.

Meanwhile, near our table, a small group had gathered, a few very pretty, lively, terribly young Asian women, each with a violin case hanging from a strap over her shoulder, grouped quietly and politely around a center that was grandly commanded by a, how can I describe this, a painterly vision, she looked like she had been sprayed into place with an atomizer, someone more like a character from the comedies of Goldoni than a person from the present century. An extravagant figure, in any case, overstepping every limit of good taste—an exclamation point!

Disneyland, docked at Venice! And there she was in full, the person whom Suvorin, when he spoke of her, only ever called "Old Schwarzberg," in a tone of voice that was somewhat untypical for him. He had once, with great ceremony, presented her with a fan to match her glasses. This was many years ago, a gift from a museumgoer paying homage to the picture he stands in front of, the portrait of a person; he adds the last little detail that was missing.

Suvorin hadn't been that far off with his somewhat Cubistic remark about the matchstick and the bulbous bowl of a pipe. He could also simply have advised me to keep an eye out for a person wearing a pair of glasses "like you've never seen before on a person's nose." She must, he guessed, have whole drawers if not dressers full of them. There they sit, on every surface in her home, a veritable museum of glasses, and still she stubbornly refuses to see anything more in this compulsion than a whim, the memory of birthdays as a child, never to be forgotten, the desire to play dress up. Was it that her skin couldn't bear any makeup? Had some young lad, eager to set himself apart from his rivals for the attention of the girl from Odessa, cut a shape out of colored paper, cleverly folded it, and then taken what he had to admit was the failed result and placed it on her youthful nose? Had she yielded to him, while the others laughed? From that point forward was every pair of glasses a symbol for her, the echo of that first, harmless, joyful profession of love?

Today she had opted for a pair with green lenses enclosed in a gold frame that curled up on the sides like dry leaves.

She had someone give her a cigarette, her whole soft rotundity swathed in an even softer yellow scarf.

Don't you dare, I admonished myself, don't you dare believe what you're seeing.

But I did believe it. I saw what Suvorin had told me about, and that he hadn't been exaggerating, not by a long shot. I saw not only the glasses, but also her earrings, the rings on her hands, and her rubber shoes, one black and one red.

That's all. Maybe, one day, if I try hard enough, I'll finally believe in the authority of what we, against our better judgment, call chance.

XIX

WHAT ELSE COULD I DO?

After being gone for a little over half a year, I came back to Vienna and called Suvorin, unsuccessfully. Since my supply of red wine was exhausted, I made a slight detour past La Gondola on my way to my wine shop—maybe, who knows, I'd find him sitting inside.

Nope, negative. Shame.

Only then did it occur to me. The old Gondola was no more. The waiters were now Croatians. They had renovated, repainted, outfitted the two rooms, which were connected by three stairs, with modern lighting. None of the old waiters I knew had been kept on, at least I didn't see any. I inquired anyway if they might know an old gentleman who often liked to stop in here, a gentleman, a character, not very tall, but strong, sturdy, a Russian, with a beard like Lenin's?

I probably shouldn't have said anything. Would they have understood me better if I had described the person I was looking for as a man who, if you put him in front of a car, any car, would be able to rip out the transmission, dismantle it, and then reinstall it from scratch?

Lenin?

The showpiece in oil that was meant to depict a city on the sea wasn't there anymore either. The Pavarotti, immortalized in black brush strokes, had likewise been mothballed. There was still pizza, as I gathered from the order being carried out from the kitchen just then. And the sign, the swoopingly erect swan's neck of a gondola that served as escutcheon, that was still here, too.

I made a second attempt, described the man I was looking for in much the way I would have to a child: that is, I was planning to send him riding across the Siberian steppe on a yak—but I never got that far. We're sorry, I was told, we're very sorry, sir! Were we talking past each other, the waiter and I? I turned away, back to the business at hand.

I'm sure the new owners didn't feel like they had been unfriendly to me; rather they suspected, I assume, that I was the one who was slow on the uptake, unable to take into consideration all the responsibilities one has to juggle after assuming control of a gastronomic enterprise. In order to at least say one hospitable thing to me (and because they had noticed my interest in the pizza), one of them pointed out that they also sold pizza to go, indeed they even delivered.

It was as if the true La Gondola had been erased; only the walls were left standing.

I said thank you and left.

Since I wasn't in a hurry, I searched the neighboring streets and alleyways, hoping for a chance run-in. The Schubert church, the pharmacy on the corner, the Turkish grocer across the street, the "Everything Specialty Store," a junk shop, the gracefully old-fashioned Vienna Chic shop that looked like a living room, the sign over the door in flowery script, the same that was painted on the shop window—it was all still here, and made me confident that Suvorin could still be here, too. What was half a year, anyway?

When it started raining, I figured I'd try the pharmacy again, waited till it was my turn in line, asked for information about the whereabouts of a friend—my first time calling him that— who had been a customer there and might still be, a Russian man. I had it down pat by now, allowed myself all manner of embellishments—though no yak, no distant peaks where only shepherds could find their way—but again met with no success, unless we count the success of being permitted to enjoy for a brief moment the blessing of a warm, professional kindness. The cucumber milk extract could wait, the pharmacist felt, and he summoned to him all the employees busy in the back room, who had worked for him for years, told them what was going on, while I, intent on furnishing every bit of pertinent information, wound up chiming in with the comment that Suvorin's upper lip and chin were adorned with a beard that reminded me of the revolutionary leader Lenin, which got a grin from the boss ("Lenin? Well, how about that!") and then, unfortunately, the same shrug as before. He would, however, he assured me, keep on the lookout for the man, I should feel free to stop in again.

The rain had gotten heavier, and I gave up.

How often did I try to get him on the telephone. I let it ring, the line wasn't dead, but no one ever picked up.

Another half a year went by, and after that years, without the man I had given a name to turning up; and I came to this part of town at least once a month and kept my eyes open. Was there no one, aside from the pharmacist, whom I could have asked about him?

Briefly the thought surfaced that he could have followed an old dream and set off for the south, headed down to the Ligurian Coast, to San Remo, where, I found myself wishing, he might now be sitting at a piano in one of the grand hotels on the sea, the Miramare Palace or the Royal San Remo, playing Gershwin in the half-light of the bar.

I had one last iron in the fire, an inquiry with the customer service department at Vienna Cemeteries GmbH, whose records, one can assume, are impeccable. No one would give me any information over the phone, they said you had to show up in person and hand over the proper paperwork. I ended up at the window of an older staffer who spoke in a broad Viennese accent and listened kindly to my request. Off she went, it becoming clear as she walked away that either her hip or her legs were giving her problems—certainly her weight was as well—and just as quickly—even, to my surprise, somewhat jauntily—she reappeared with documents under her arm. She beamed at me, showing the laugh lines on her face, and I grew hopeful. She was sorry, she said, among those deceased in Vienna in the time frame we were looking at, no one was listed under the name I had given. A Suvorina, yes, a Suvorin, no. Incidentally, the files showed that someone was behind on payment of a few outstanding bills connected to the gravesite for this Suvorina. And the letters we've sent, reminders, have gone unanswered, though they haven't been returned either. We even sent one of our colleagues after him, someone who knows Russian.

What graciousness. What could I come up with, how could I manage to get her beaming at me again, showing the laugh lines on her face? But I didn't have to do a thing. She took a piece of candy from a bowl and handed it to me—and beamed.

I rode the tram back to the city along the Ring, past the massive State Opera, past Heldenplatz. Once I got back home, I threw myself onto the bed and lit a cigarette. Everything about him that had once been alive, and now had gone dark, had become a mystery—it remained a riddle. What else could I do? In looking for Suvorin, I felt like I was disturbing the peaceful repose of a dead man who, in life, had been no more than a stranger to me.

As I lay on the bed and said my farewells, I remembered that exquisitely friendly woman at the cemetery office, who had spoken of letters that they had sent to Suvorin—which meant that she must be in possession of a valid address. I could . . . yes, I could, I should try to ask her to do me the favor of letting me have it. Only then would the balance of my search for Suvorin be settled. I didn't doubt that my request would be successful, but something in me resisted. I saw myself looking for a building and stepping inside, saw myself climbing the stairs, standing at the door to an apartment, waiting for a sound, a sign of life, and what else? A handshake with a dead man?

This much was clear, it would take courage to actually do the thing, to announce myself by ringing or knocking or calling out, a courage that I, knowing myself as I do, wouldn't be able to muster. When it comes to death, I'm a coward. The idea that his heart had stopped beating, that he could be lying dead in his apartment, shriveled, dried out—it depressed me. The mere thought of it made me nervous, that I could be guilty of disturbing him, of imposing in a way that he, were he to find me standing at his door, would certainly see as inappropriate and so take offense. Was I entitled to feel worried?

Where were his children?

Just thinking about it made me sad and discouraged.

No, I decided. And I was afraid.

Now the question might arise as to whether the man I was thinking about ever existed, or whether he might not have been a ghost, a phantom, from the first moment on, when I met him in the coffeehouse.

Such creatures exist, even in the coffeehouses of Vienna, in the outer districts more than in the city center. It's best to believe that the people who just stood up from your table, cocked their hats, and vanished out the door will no longer be a part of your life, because they were never even a part of their own. Phantoms! Maybe, if you're a good dreamer, you'll meet them in your sleep, in a dream that doesn't want anything from you.

That's how it was with me. I didn't think of him for years. I had, I thought, forgotten him.

But every now and then I would experience a moment of shock, a brief instant, fully unexpected, that would stop me in my tracks and, when I turned to look closer, left me terribly upset. Even more than the thought that flashed through my mind, what upset me was the shame at even thinking of the possibility of encountering him one day as a poor unfortunate, a tramp, a beggar, a homeless man. Missing! How sure I was of doing wrong by him, the man sleeping in a subway car, the stooped man with the hat pulled down over his face, the poor wretch with the full beard, hardly recognizable, the man with a flask in his pocket, always within reach, and a cardboard cup in his hands, folded together and imploring, empty but for a few coins?

Distraught, I hurried off.

But then, suddenly, there he was again. There he was, unmistakably Suvorin, taking the seat next to mine at the coffeehouse with his very unkempt and slightly comical Lenin goatee. I can say I recognized him. His laugh, too, was his own (did Lenin ever laugh?). A dream, as fast as a spinning wheel, no music, not a word about music, no piano in sight. There was no audience, I can't remember a single person watching when I fell asleep.

The late-afternoon light got gloomier with every stroke of the cathedral bell. The small alleys wound and curved. It was snowing, the wind whipped the snowflakes against the tall windows. More calamity than weather. All of Vienna hung crooked on its hinges.

Communism, said the man, left no proof that it had ever existed on our planet. Yes, that's what his voice had sounded like, just like that, muted, hindered by shortness of breath. I barely understood him when he talked, nor did I understand what he was talking about, what its connection was with us, our being there. But please, what does a dream care about connections, what does it care if I get disoriented. And what does Suvorin care! Rarely did he develop a thought from its beginning to its middle and on through to the end. Into one thought crept others, scraps, fragments, also little hesitations that weren't really caused by him pausing to think, but were rather the result of (a) his once-excessive drinking (long-term consequences); (b) many years of prolonged interaction with the content of modern musical scores, i.e., dissonances; (c) acute circulatory difficulties; (d) progressively poorer digestion; (e) his innate disregard for any kind of order (soldiers marching in formation hadn't impressed him even as a child!) and for the question of which year, decade, or even century a given notion owed its provenance; and (f) his unapologetically strong appreciation for nonsense, even at his age, and his belief in its utility. That'll do, I think.

Well, all right, one more. Never say what you think, especially not in a dictatorship. That's for sure. There's always somebody scratching at your door, even if he just wants to ask after your mother's health. Why do you think I smoked like a chimney back then? Why Dmitri turned into a chain smoker under Stalin? Why people, educated people who knew how to express themselves, suddenly started stuttering and couldn't get a word out? Why poems were so popular? And those who wrote them? With a wit worthy of a poet, Kovalev wrote that the Revolution was the inventor of a chair that nobody could sit on.

I felt lost.

What does exist are its crimes. It's the great contributions I'm still waiting to hear about. They have lies on their conscience, great patriotic lies, the lies of peace and war. They declared death their ally, disposed of people with a shot in the back of the head, slowly beat them to death, sentenced them to an even slower death by forced labor. A scream passed through every victim, an orchestra played, a mouthful of bread for their payment, a reprieve before they, too, were liquidated. Men, women, children.

My God! Was he a dream himself, appearing before me in a dream like this? Was my dream what he had filmed with his camera? Filmed himself, added his own voice to the soundtrack, with the soothingly dark timbre it took on only when he spoke his mother tongue? Hadn't he said that at some point he would have to get hold of a tripod that he could mount the camera on?

The actor waves from across a field, amid the flowers in the open air. By now, I was searching, once more the deeply conscientious youth who, even in his school days, and then all the more so from his first years of college onward, had been inspired by the free thinking of the early philosophers—searching for a clear description of what is meant by the words *spirit, phantom, ghost,* or related phenomena; I took notes about it—a little pedantic, I'll admit. Even after waking I couldn't get to the bottom of what it all means, how easy it is to write when you don't do it sitting down, on paper, with letters.

He looked over my shoulder, amused. How about this: A stranger comes to the city.

A familiar opening.

The main thing is for the story to begin on a day like any of the days we've known.

Right, but something is still off.

The visible conceals the invisible.

Like even numbers conceal the odd, like a fan conceals a face?

A movie star, female, a big icon, in an interview: "I'm only a beautiful woman when nobody's looking."

In the next trailer a man, revolver in one hand, script in the other, is reading the same line over and over again: "I know why I love you!" What he doesn't know is how he should say it. He still doesn't have a feeling for the tone, for the lie, as it turns out in the end. He knows the plot. For him, it's not at all about loving or being loved. The line sounds best, he finds, if he says it very slowly, while staring at his gun, since that's what it is that he really loves.

I had stopped being surprised.

The bride in the prettiest dress! A coal-black cat on the roof of a parked car. My mystery is an old man, Hollywood's not interested, coffee is served.

Let's end the story where it began, in that coffeehouse on that once-quiet little side street where, long ago, I used to like to pass the time, often whole days at a stretch, in fact. Nowadays of course it's become even more famous than it was already, than it was, really, from the start—and well, it hasn't done it any good, I don't think. The tobacco smoke has cleared out, and the artists with it. It's hard to bring yourself to address the waiters with the old-fashioned but still everywhere prevalent *Herr Ober*. They belong to a generation that, as Suvorin once remarked, never had a straw in their mouth that had been made of actual straw.

There is nothing to indicate that he ever eats anything of nutritional value. Yes, coffee, for sure, with a glass of water, but without sugar: a single course, arranged on a silver platter, served like a meal.

Right now everything requires the utmost concentration, which means everything will come in due time. The day's going to pass by somehow!

The coffee flowed drop by drop into the prewarmed cup, and in the same way, drop by drop, he drinks the coffee down. He puckers his lips like a flautist, it's just that the sound that we hear isn't a flute, it's a whistle, not loud, not even unpleasant, a breath, breathing in the smallest possible quantity.

His tongue, curved like a spoon, receives the first drop, sucks it up—a joy, what joy such things can bring.